I0545715

THE SEA-FIEND;

OR,

THE ABBOT OF ST. MARK'S.

A Legendary Romance.

BY GEORGE DIBDEN PITT.

Why do I yield to that suggestion,
Whose horrid image doth unfix my brain,
And make my seated heart knock at my ribs
Against the use of nature.—*Macbeth.*

LONDON:
PUBLISHED BY E. LLOYD, 12, SALISBURY-SQUARE, FLEET-STREET.

1846.

THE SEA-FIEND;
OR, THE ABBOT OF ST. MARK'S.
A Legendary Romance.

BY GEORGE DIBDIN PITT.

CHAPTER I.

A MAN of retired habits, a poet, and a lover of literature in all its branches, to whom we will give the name of Fenrose, such being his travelling cognomen, during the latter part of a hot summer, took up his residence at Sandwich, in Kent. Its ancient appearance, and its vicinity to monuments of antiquity, suited well with his humour : Sandwich gives to a traveller the idea of the fortified cities of the olden time. Its thick walls, moat, and drawbridge, inspire an awe, as he enters the town from Margate. It is a place of no traffic, and in the very meridian of day, a cannon might be fired up the principal street without any fear of the ball striking any one. Yet it is a pleasant little place, and the inhabitants kindly and hospitable—so Fenrose found them, and I believe all who ever entered its time-honoured walls.

On the cliff above, or immediately adjoining, stands Richborough Castle, the first Roman station in this island, and such the strength of the materials, and the solidity of the buildings, that neither time nor the efforts of man have been able to destroy it. The party on whose ground it stands, finding it occupy so large a space of his land, has repeatedly tried to raze it to the ground; but, as Roderick Dhu, in "The Lady of the Lake," observes, as easy may you try "to move Benleden from his staunce," as to break through its mighty walls.

In this venerable ruin Fenrose passed a great part of his time, his mind, on imagination's wing, reverting back to the time when the mighty Roman warrior, Julius Cæsar, sat in its capacious hall, and the centurion watched upon its towers. Again would his mind revert to the bold Norman baron and his lady-bride, seated on the dais, with their retainers ranged at the tables beneath; when the red deer and huge boar's head formed the chief dishes at a British banquet: then would he think also of the time when the "preux chevalier" reigned in the crusader's hall, and wine and wassail gave place to more refined manners and customs; but the object which most engaged his attention, was the watery plain, partly sand, and part coarse grass and mud, through which were paths, and a road made from Ramsgate to Sandwich. The spot to which I am alluding, is close to the latter; it bears the appearance of a neglected churchyard—innumerable barrows and mounds intersecting each other in rows. Beneath this lay the city or town of Stoner, that shared the fate of the kingdom or earldom of Mercia, now buried beneath the Goodwin Sands, being swallowed up by the sea at a more recent period. Historians differ as to the exact date, but such was the fate of a populous city, engulphed in a moment by the ocean. The mighty wave came on, overwhelming all—no time was allowed for preparation, and a whole people were destroyed at once. In the lapse of ages the sea has again receded, leaving devoted Stonar buried fathoms deep in sand and shingle.

Beneath the castle wall, in the moonlight, did Fenrose love to recline, gazing on the silvery wave, and on the site of the ocean city—the mounds and barrows forming, to his eye, the traces of streets and buildings, and letting his imagination run on its devoted inhabitants. One evening, wandering through the castle ruin, he seated himself in the hall, where now a large blackthorn grows, where once stood the festive board, and Roman conquerors' cuirel chair. On the remains of a fallen pillar he sat, leaning his cheek upon his hand, and was soon lost in an intense reverie.

While thus absorbed, the solemn silence of the place, and the heat yet left of an overpowering day, caused sleep to steal upon him till he was lost in slumber. Though his eyes were closed, and the heart slept, still the mind, that "wondrous mind of man," yet worked, and creative imagination gave birth in sleep to wondrous dreams. Suddenly, from the thorn before mentioned, a man in a monastic habit, of the class of a superior, and whose countenance exhibited a horrid mixture of demoniac feelings and terror, stood before him. His scapulary was fringed with locks of the raven hue; and his eye-brows, of the same colour, scowled fearfully on him. In his hand he held a roll of papers. He stood motionless, yet seemed as though he fain would speak, and yet was doubtful. Starting from his seat, Fenrose surveyed the intruder with alarm and awe. He felt he stood before a supernatural being. Summoning resolution, however, he accosted him.

"Who, and what art thou," he said, "that thus at midnight traverse these time-honoured ruins? Say, art thou a being like myself, who delights in solitudes and silence? or art thou the shade of one whose soul is doomed yet to wander through the scenes of bye-gone days? Speak, I charge you, in the name of the Most High."

A deep groan burst from the spectre, as though his form was yet agonized by human feelings, and in a hollow sepulchral tone it answered,—

" You have done wisely, and him you have invoked hath given you grace and strength to speak. I am, as thou sayest, a spirit, doomed to wander. I was once a denizen of devoted Stonar, for my crimes condemned to wake in woe while a lost people sleep in eternal rest. None know the history of that ill-fated city, or the horror of that dreadful night which consigned a people to a watery grave, unprepared, unanealed, cut off in an instant, and called before an angry God. But what were they compared to me? The very fiends refuse to fraternize with me, or admit me to a partnership of torment—for their tortures will cease, and, their sad probation past, they will also rest in peace; but I must wander in realms of eternal silence, with the bandog, conscience, for ever gnawing at my heart, in agonies unspeakable, to warn others, in generations yet to come. I have here penned an account of my life and crimes, and with it the history of Stonar's fate; take it, and in thy dream peruse the wondrous tale; so shall Heaven strengthen thy memory, that though the visionary MS. vanish from thy grasp, thy brain retain its records, for thee afresh to pen, and instruct a wondering world."

So saying, the sprite extended its arm, and placing the manuscript in the hand of Fenrose, slowly vanished from his sight. For several moments the poet stood wrapt in amazement, until the opening of a door close to him made him turn quickly round, when to his surprise he observed a portal, hitherto obscured by brambles and ivy, stand open, from which streamed the light of a flambeau. Making his way over the grass-grown flooring of the hall, in some trepidation, Fenrose entered the apartment, which he soon perceived was perfectly untenanted. It was a large vaulted chamber, used, in days of yore, as a retiring room or hall of private audience. In the centre was a massive oak table, and chairs of antique form and workmanship; from the vaulted roof, which was carved in the ancient gothic style, by a brass chain, hung a lamp of the same metal, embossed with figures in the Roman costume; an exceeding bright light emanated from it, which shone on the table and the space around, though it failed to illumine the heavy oaken panels of its walls. On the back of the chair was carved the S P Q R of Rome, and a brazen eagle, richly gilt, extended its wings on the top of it; the fasces, or axe and rods, of the lictors ornamented its arms, which were also richly gilt. The apartment was strewn with rushes, and had the appearance of recent usage. For some time Fenrose contemplated it in silence. The door he had entered by closed of itself; placing the manuscript on the table, he sat himself down. He doubted not but that he sat in the very chair, and in the very " sanctum " of the conqueror of Europe and Africa—that Cæsar whose name can never die. He felt a reverential awe steal over his senses; it seemed as though Philippi's ghost then hovered nigh. Collecting himself, and remembering the words of the spectre, he unrolled the manuscript, which ran thus:—

The Confessions of the Abbot of St. Mark.

Hoarse howled the tempest, and sullenly boomed the waves against the rocks that begirt the shores of Stonar, as Albert Durand drew near to its embattled wall. The gates were closed, and the warder from the parapet refused all entrance till sunrise. Cold, and rain-drenched, Albert looked wistfully around in quest of some habitation where he might obtain shelter. High above the city frowned the Castle of Richborough in haughty grandeur, as though it yet held the men, " whom the groans of the despairing Britons implored to guard and save them from the ferocious Dane."

The monastery of St. Mark, the principal building in Stonar, tenanted by the monks of the order of St. Dominick, gave notice of the hour of twelve. The heart of Albert sank as the iron tongue of time vibrated on his ear; yet sadder far were his thoughts as he raised his eye to the dim outline of Richborough Castle, in the foggy air, as it stood in bold relief against the sky. Again he looked towards the ocean, and as the waves broke upon the shore, beneath their curling tops demoniac faces seemed to gleam and frown on the devoted wanderer; the shriek of the mermaid was heard as she fled from the ocean kelpie, and the seagull echoed back the cry.

At that moment his eye caught the glimmer of a light in a habitation under the walls ; it proceeded from the humble dwelling of a tailor, known for his industry and eccentricity, who, like many others, found it suited his finances better to lodge without the walls than to pay the high rents demanded for the domiciles within. To this man's dwelling Albert directed his steps, though so late an hour. Pierce Gherkin, the little tailor, yet toiled, upon something like a carpenter's bench, which served for table, counter, and shopboard—for the tailor dealt in more ways than one at that time of day. He was then busy in completing the repairs of a huge pair of inexpressibles—in those days, and of the material of those days, no trifling affair.

On Albert's knocking at the door with the hilt of his trusty sword, the little tailor started from his oriental posture, and shrouding the lamp with his hands, cowered beneath his shopboard (Heaven bless the mark) ! Applying his face to the window, Albert tapped lightly at it, at the same time calling to the little repairer of damaged weeds by his name, for Pierce was known to him, though he never knew before the place of his abode. The well-known voice reassured Gherkin, who quickly opened his door to the wet and wearied Albert.

"My certes," quoth Pierce, as he replaced the massy bar, "who would have thought of seeing Master Albert Durand at such a time ; but the devil never loses himself—begging your pardon for the proverb. You'll be cold and hungry, I suppose." So saying, Pierce placed a log of wood and some turfs on the "dogs," as the grate or bars were then termed, consisting of a bar of iron with two claws or supporters at each end ; this stood about a foot or less from the hearth, and against it were piled the turf and wood. Thus low, and the seats placed in the wide and ample chimney-nook, the term of "sitting over the fire" was strictly correct—the figure of speech still remains—though the improvement and formation of modern grates and chimney ranges cause us now to sit "before the fire." In the chimney corner of the olden time, in the house of Gherkin, the tailor, did Albert Durand extend his limbs, while Pierce busied himself in preparing for his guest's supper—an arrangement soon made, for the contents of the larder were trifling, consisting of some brown bread, a small hock of bacon, or rather the bone—for little more remained—and a piece of poor cheese ; this, with some brandy, obtained from the hardy coasters, and kept by the little tailor as a recipe for lowness of spirits, was the sum total of Gherkin's means of entertainment ; and, poor as it might seem, it was acceptable to Albert, and, aided by the genial glow of the fire, restored animation to his benumbed limbs. While despatching his humble meal, he questioned Pierce as to Richborough and its proud castellan, Baron Fitzormond.

"Ah! Master Albert, sad changes since you left Stonar for France—the baron has grown so moody that his vassals dread to approach him. His daughter, the Lady Sabina, is not suffered to stir beyond the drawbridge, and a sentinel continually attends upon her steps. Marry, the times are sadly changed, good Master Albert," continued Pierce, "since I fitted you with your first hunting tunic of Lincoln green, when you rode on the Shetland pony beside my lord."

A deep sigh burst from Albert, in confirmation of the tailor's remark, who proceeded thus,—

" That same Richborough Castle is enough to give his lordship, the baron, the horrors and the blue devils ; the place is as full of ghosts as a whaler is of rats. Every night, they say, the Roman cohorts come marching to the castle gates, and clash their swords against their bucklers ; and then the last Friday in every month, just as the clock gives notice of the midnight hour, Sir Brian Braose, the Norman, who was the castellan in the time of William the Conqueror, is seen to drag his fair daughter by her beautiful hair down the great staircase, and out of the great gate, under the portcullis and over the drawbridge, and on to the cliff, and there a yellow-haired Saxon youth meets him, and is killed by the baron, who then throws his daughter over the cliff, and there she is struggling with the waves ; and then a pack of fiends, like greyhounds, with terrible heads, pursue him into the castle ; and the lady screams, and the baron curses, and the dog-fiends howl, and course him through every room in the place till three o'clock, and then all's quiet again."

Thus did the garrulous tailor run on, and further had he carried his wondrous account, but that an impatient interjection from Albert stayed him in the very torrent of his speech.

" Can you believe such nonsense ?" said Albert.

" No, not I, in faith," answered the tailor; " I don't believe either that or the story of the black boar covered with blood, that runs through the great gallery just at twilight; or about the terrible Ocean Fiend, that every new year's eve comes out of the wave, all glittering in silver scales, and claps his fins, and laughs, and cries, ' But a little while, and then !' Then he's interrupted by such a shriek, that seems to come out of the sea, as though all the poor souls that ever were drowned, were calling for help, and he dives down to quiet them, and is never seen till the next year. But, howsomever, that is true, because the Lady Sabina Fitzormond saw him from her turret window."

Pushing the platter impatiently from him, Albert desired Pierce never to couple the name of Lady Sabina with so monstrous a fiction, which, though he lived in the dark age of superstition, Albert could give no credence to. Complaining then of drowsiness, he was shown by the hospitable little tailor to a chamber. Pierce, after setting down the lamp and pointing to the couch, would fain have renewed his catalogue of wonders, but that the weariness of his guest forbid; so bidding him " good morning," it having passed the midnight period so considerably, he left him to his dreams and meditations.

Ridiculous as the story seemed, the last fiction of the Ocean Fiend seemed to haunt Albert's mind, probably from the name of Lady Sabina being brought in in confirmation, for that name was never mentioned without exciting strong emotion in the heart of Durand. Previous to throwing himself on the couch, he opened the latticed casement of his chamber and looked out. It was November, and still dark; the air, unlike the refreshing morning breeze of summer, was cold and bleak; the sky covered or obscured by thick murky clouds, whose quick sailing motion gave token of a boisterous morrow. The waves seemed to curl their high tops as though they would gather strength to dash the opposing rocks to pieces—an unusual swell pervaded the bosom of the ocean; high upon the wing was heard the osprey, screaming as though it " scented the tempest from afar;" the little city, or town—for in those days the distinction was not so great, neither were cities so large—of Stonar seemed lost in the shadow of the cliff. He looked towards the south turret; a light was perceptible in a window—it was the Lady Sabina's apartment. He knew the window well, for full many a night had he robbed nature of her dues to keep watchful vigil there, in the hope of detecting but a glimpse of her fair form; those times were past, and hope revisited his heart no more. Sighing deeply, he withdrew his gaze from the turret, and fixed them on the beach, which, being chiefly composed of shingle, seemed in constant motion as it was washed by the ever-coming wave. A dark form stood motionless, and, though at that distance, seemed as though it gazed on Albert. Thus it stood for some moments; it then extended its right arm to Stonar, then pointed with the left towards the ocean. Albert was now convinced he was himself the object of the figure's regard. It now seemed slowly to recede towards the sea. The moon, struggling to assert her rights, partly dispelled a portion of her black and billowing foes, and sailing bereft of half her bright refulgence, cast a sickly gleam upon the shore; and immediately upon the mysterious form. Like the tench, whose scales are black and gold, as its varying motion meets the light, so did the black form glitter in the moonbeam, and yet stood darkly terrible. An overwhelming wave came rushing on the shore, gathering the shallow waters round; the figure appeared to move towards it, yet still, though distance and darkness forbid Albert to distinguish features, it seemed to gaze on him. The billow top curled high in silvery canopy above its head; black as the ebon sceptre of Erebus the demi-demon stood; then, like the silvery flash of the shark, dazzling the eye as it turns to seize its victim, it seemed glittering in emerald brightness, as the wave, bursting over it, hid it from the sight. The grey dawn was at the moment seen through the thin light clouds, and the cock's shrill clarion gave notice of the coming day.

Albert passed his hand over his eyes, and could scarce convince himself that he was really awake again. He looked towards the beach—not a vestige of the figure was to be seen; conceiving it to be the creation of a brain jaded and excited by fatigue and bitter reflections, and closing the casement, he threw himself upon the couch, and humble as the accommodations were, he was soon lost in a profound slumber, undisturbed by startling dreams.

While Albert Durand tastes the last tranquil repose he ever knew in this world, the reader shall be made acquainted with his early history.

The father of Albert Durand had been a faithful vassal and adherent of Gervas, the former baron, uncle to Rowland Fitzormond, the present castellan, and saved the life of his lord in battle; but in so doing received so severe a wound, that he expired in a few days after, bequeathing Albert, his only son, then an orphan, to the care of the baron, who pledged his knightly word to be a parent to him. Albert after the funeral, therefore, took up his abode in the castle; but, while yet a boy, lost his first protector, who, with his dying breath, recommended him to the care of Rowland, whose page he became, and who treated him with the same uniform kindness that his uncle had ever done; the baroness, too, treated him more as a son than a dependant; and the Lady Sabina, a child but a few years younger than himself, loved him with the affection of a sister. As he grew up he was taught to ride the " great horse," as the Saracen breed of war-steeds was called; he was instructed in arms and archery, and also in all the clerkly accomplishments of the age. Though not admitted on a footing at the festive board, in all things else did he enjoy so high a privilege, that a stranger visitant would have deemed him some distant relative or child of a cherished friend, rather than the offspring of a serf. He was the friend and playmate of Sabina, her faithful guard and champion; deep was the attachment in either heart, and thus passed youth's early day, till the young were amazed to find themselves no longer children.

As yet, they were ignorant that they were cherishing a guilty flame. They were first awoke to a sense of its impropriety by an accident that occurred to Albert, when hunting with his lord. The horse on which the youth rode—a creature of approved metal, and so attached to its youthful rider, that when he was mounted on the faithful creature she seemed to pay attention to his very thought—like the Centaur, they seemed as forming but one being—in the height of the chase, just as he was taking a most dangerous leap, which nothing but a firm reliance in her metal could warrant, the creature, in the act of springing, received a blow on the face with a stone, thrown from an unseen hand, and so violent, that the animal fell back on her haunches, and fairly rolled over her rider. Albert was taken up senseless and covered with blood; by the baron's order, he was immediately carried back to the castle on a litter, and a messenger despatched for the most experienced and competent leech that Canterbury could produce. Ere his arrival Albert had recovered, and all fears of an inward bruise entirely dissipated by his asserting that he felt not the slightest inconvenience from the effects of the fall, being only alarmed for the generous animal that he had ridden.

Every inquiry was made, and a strict investigation entered into as to how the stone came to strike the horse, and by whom thrown, but without the least success. He was beloved by all the domestics and retainers too much for any of them to have been guilty of such an act; it was, therefore, deemed to be the action of some miscreant unknown; the baron causing strict search to be made in the forest and the villages around.

When Albert was brought into the castle covered with blood, and dying, as it was feared, the baroness and the whole household expressed great grief and alarm, but the anguish and concern of Sabina exceeded all limits—she shrieked, tore her hair, threw herself upon his bleeding form, and was with difficulty removed to her chamber and pacified. When he recovered, and went to remove the fears of the baroness, and thank her for her solicitude, Sabina, who was with her, and who had sent every moment to inquire after him, started from her seat and throwing her arms round his neck, kissed him in fond solicitude, and wept upon his shoulder; nor was he less affected. The baroness in a moment saw how negligent and unthinking she had been, and resolved to put a stop to that which, encouraged longer, might lead to disastrous results. Rising from her seat, she sharply reproved Sabina, and bade her follow her instantly to her bower, or chamber—in modern times styled boudoir. In terror and surprise Sabina slowly obeyed, leaving Albert astonished and alarmed.

Still this was but unsophisticated nature; our first parents in their earlier moments had not purer thoughts; this the baroness believed. She loved her daughter, she was partial to Albert, but she saw it was necessary to take steps to prevent a repetition of such scenes, and, like too many other parents, she took the wrong steps. The love of a parent for her child, and her solicitude for its welfare, is beautiful, 'tis sublime; yet 'tis but a step from the sublime to the ridiculous, and how often does the mistaken affection of parents verge on the ridiculous.

"A cunning fellow, yet ignorant, confessing to the priest, was asked what calling he followed, and on his informing the monk that he officiated as a groom or horsekeeper, the worthy ecclesiastic, not being satisfied at his very limited list of offences, asked him if he ever stole his master's hay or corn—thereby cheating his employer, and defrauding the poor animals; to all he pleaded not guilty; the priest then asked if he ever greased the teeth of the horses, to prevent them from eating, thereby finding a ready excuse for taking the allotted food from them. 'Did you ever do this?' asked the priest.

"'No,' said the clown, 'for I never know'd that greasing the teeth would prevent the horses from eating; I'm obliged to you for telling me.'" The tale is a homely one, but the application is just. Parents and guardians of every denomination, in their mistaken style of preventing youth from committing errors, actually put them on the scent, and give them the zest, themselves.

Asking pardon for this digression, I will pursue my story.

The severe lecture which the baroness gave Sabina, and the picture she painted of the evils attendant upon disobedience, and consequent on improper connexions, opened the eyes of her daughter to a sense of her natural, yet improper display of solicitude so much, that she might properly be said to have become a woman from that moment. When next she met Albert, though she inquired after his health with condescending kindness, yet there was a restraint, a reserve, with which she checked his advances, and even looks, that mortified him, and made him truly miserable.

Among the friendships that he had contracted in his own sphere, there was a youth, the head falconer's son, to whom he had ever shown the greatest preference, until at last they became inseparables—the Castor and Pollux of Kent; yet no two beings could be more opposite than Albert Durand and Arnold Moseley. Arnold was the elder by two years; a difference which in advanced manhood is as nothing, but in youth affording a marked advantage. Albert was considered an exceeding handsome youth; Arnold, hard-featured and forbidding; Albert was open, generous, and confiding, but hasty and passionate; Arnold, on the contrary, was close, mean, and reserved; Albert, from being so far exalted above his fellows, and enjoying such unlimited power, without knowing it himself, had an air of hauteur that gave him the appearance of a scion of the aristocracy, more than a dependant; Arnold was mean and cringing to his superiors, and affected a bland and affable bearing to all,—he was surely hypocrisy identified and embodied; such was the youth who had wormed himself into the confidence of Albert, and such the difference of their two characters. To Arnold he flew, when he perceived the change in Sabina's manner, and that of the baroness, to impart his woes.

The other heard him with much seeming concern, yet inwardly exulted, envying Albert the high place he held in the baron's favour. He secretly practised every art and scheme to undo him, nor had he scrupled to endeavour to obtain his end by the worst means. His hand it was that hurled the stone at the horse's head, and caused the accident. He had secreted himself in a thicket close by; he had marked the course of the deer, and knew the horsemen would have the leap to take at that spot. The result is known—he immediately made a detour, and appearing to come up breathless, affected the utmost concern at the accident.

He played the distracted friend so well that no one could suspect him as the guilty party. He had hoped that Albert was indeed killed, and was truly mortified at his recovery; and even a greater cause for hatred had he. He cherished in secret a guilty passion for the Lady Sabina, and her marked partiality to Albert was in itself sufficient for hatred to him; and when he heard of his present rebuff, he joyed in the youth's distress. Still did he dissemble so well, and pretend such a friendly concern, that the deceived Albert hugged himself in the idea of having such a friend. By the advice of Arnold, he wrote to her in private, and an interview took place, which sealed the fate of the unhappy pair. He forgot all his wise resolutions he had made, and falling on his knee, poured forth his soul in strains of love. She confessed her attachment, and they parted, the most happy and most wretched pair in Christendom. Arnold was an unseen witness of all. At twilight, and in early morn, they met, and seemed but to live in each others' society. This went on for a time, and though their attachment could not but be noticed by those who knew them, they vainly flattered themselves that they were undiscovered, as the ostrich, hiding its head, deems itself safe from its pursuers, because it sees not them.

The period had now arrived that Arnold had waited for. He had lulled them into a fatal security. He now, by ambiguous hints and mysterious mutterings, attracted the baron's notice, who demanded the reason. At first Arnold affected unwillingness, then fear, and at length having wrought the baron to the utmost pitch, fell on his knees, implored his lordship's pardon for thus long concealing it from his knowledge, spoke in terms of the highest praise of Albert, then pretended to weep for him, and the imprudence of his young lady, and then, with well-affected ingenious candour, informed the wrathful father of all their meetings, and where they then were conversing together in a small plantation near the castle. Drawing his sword, and commanding Arnold and two other vassals to attend him, the enraged Fitzormond took his way to the plantation, where but too surely the unconscious pair were exchanging vows of mutual fidelity. Sabina urged the danger of discovery, while Arnold as warmly urged her to quit the castle, and fly with him.

"Leave my dear parents!" cried Sabina; "it would break my loved mother's heart. I never could meet their anger—I should live in continual terror, and sink prematurely to the grave, with a father's curse upon my head."

Seizing her hand, and sinking on his knee,—

"Beloved Sabina," cried Albert, "I will be parent, brother, lover, husband, all. We will fly to another land—in time the baron will relent, and we shall return in happiness. Sabina, my love, my soul, my wife!"

Her head sunk upon his shoulder, while tears relieved the overfraught heart. In wild rapture his lips pressed her blushing cheek. At that moment a voice like thunder startled them, and the baron stood before them. In an agony of terror the devoted girl sunk on her knees. Not for herself she pleaded, but for him whose peril she shuddered to think of. The enraged Fitzormond cut short her faltering appeal, and loaded her with curses and execrations. Shocked at his manner of upbraiding the gentle girl, and blaming himself for being the cause of placing her in such a situation, Albert expostulated with the baron, and begged to be heard.

"Drag the villain to the deepest dungeon of the keep, beneath the level of the sea!" roared Fitzormond.

Albert was seized, and his arms pinioned on the instant. Fearful of further violence, Sabina attempted to step between her lover and enraged father. The baron's fury now knew no bounds. Seizing his wretched daughter by her flowing hair, he dragged her fainting into the castle, where she was saved from further ill-usage by the baroness, who hurried her to her chamber, where she was made a close prisoner.

Albert struggled violently to free himself from his guards, that he might rescue Sabina from her father, whom he feared would murder her, but in vain. He was conducted unceremoniously into the dungeon, according to the baron's orders; a horrid place, far removed from air, or light of day. An iron girdle was put round his waist, to which was attached a ponderous chain. A little straw was the only bed he had to repose on, which Arnold, who pretended to sympathise with him,

See page 8.

brought in as an act of friendship. He denied to Albert all knowledge of tht baron's intention, and the too credulous youth believed the villain to be the trues and best of friends. Placing the lamp they had brought with them on a stone raised for that purpose, the three left him. Arnold whispered as he passed out,—
"Sabina—escape. Rely on your friend."

The iron studded door shut them from his view, and he felt himself alone, a miserable prisoner deep in the bowels of the earth, from which he never might emerge again. If it was the baron's intention to take his life, here he could be murdered, and none ever made acquainted with his fate; and in those days, the murder of a vassal (unless under very aggravated circumstances, and with some influential person to bring the case forward) was rarely noticed.

Throwing himself upon the straw, he cursed his fate, and groaned in agony of heart; he pressed his hot and throbbing temples to the cold flag-stones to assuage his pain; he tried to sleep, but in vain. He cast his eyes round his cheerless abode; it was small, and the vaulted arch was lost in gloom, for the lamp wanted trimming, and they had forgotten to supply it with oil; he now saw that his misery might yet be augmented, for, in a few minutes, he should be in utter darkness—a state fearful to the human mind under any circumstances. He rose, and walked to and fro, as far as his chain would permit him, in the most wretched state of mind, fears for Sabina overcoming all selfish feelings; yet her parents were sure to forgive her in time, and the sooner, were he for ever removed.

At this moment the light expired; though he had anticipated the event, still, when it did happen, his heart sank within him. Making his way to the straw, he sat himself down, and leaned his back against the damp wall; here, for a time, he moralized upon the past, till he sank into a deep slumber.

When he awoke, for a few seconds he marvelled where he was; but the sad reality soon presented itself. How long he had slept, he knew not; he listened, but no sound met his ear, except the sharp squeak of the rat as it sported with its kind. How could the creatures subsist in those dungeons and passages? the thoughts made him revert to his own wants, for he felt the gnawing within, which convinced him that he had slept longer than he had at first deemed. Was it night or morning? did they mean to destroy him by starvation? At that moment a slight sound struck upon his ear; he listened—he thought it seemed louder—he scarcely dared to breathe, yet he could distinguish footsteps—they were coming, then. A key was now put into the lock; he expected every minute to see the door open, when suddenly the steps receded again, and he could plainly hear the footsteps die away in the distance. Was this to torment him? the most degraded captive had bread and water, with a light to cheer him. Again the conflicting crowd of thoughts gave way to sleep, and again he awoke a prey to the most fearful torments—a burning thirst, the gnawing of hunger was now succeeded by a sickening faintness; he must have slept many hours— the silence and darkness having encouraged the feeling.

Two days must have passed; he tried to rise from the floor—he could not move—he seemed fastened down to the floor. Was it weakness? Alas! some spell was on him, and he soon must cease to breathe; he, therefore, endeavoured to prepare himself for death: and now a low noise as of a rumbling was heard at a distance; he listened, but hope was dead within him.

After a time, it was certain that several persons were advancing; he now endeavoured to call out, but his voice seemed gone, his tongue clove to the roof of his mouth, he could not articulate a sound; the key was heard to turn in the rusty wards, and two men with a torch entered the room: one had a weight on his shoulders, which he set down; they were the two men that had seized him and brought him to the cell. Recognizing them, he in a low voice said,—

"Stephen."

The man started, and, looking at Albert, who sat with his back leaned against the churlish stones that composed the sides of his dungeon, he hastily lowered the torch to have a more perfect view of his face—the man staggered back.

"Walter!" he cried to his fellow, " a ghost—a ghost! it moves and speaks. He's come again, by all the blessed saints."

" You are a fool," surlily growled the other, who had just deposited his burden in the corner, and taking up the torch which the other had in his terror let fall, and passing the light before his eyes, said, " Dash me, if the youth ain't alive! What the deuce were you and Arnold drunk, to deceive my lord in this manner? How came you two to assert that he was dead?"

Albert now made known to them his situation, and begged them to tell him how long he had been there, entreating piteously for water and a morsel of bread.

The man first named, Stephen, immediately betook himself out of the dungeon; Walter, the other man, informed Albert that this was the seventh day of his imprisonment; that Arnold had been with food, and found him dead, and that he had by the baron's order made a coffin, pointing at the same time to the burden he had placed in the corner, where a veritable shell was indeed standing, adding, " It's well you thought fit to come to yourself now, youngster, or in another quarter of an hour you would have been boxed up, and safe in the monks' burying-ground, where your grave is now dug, by the abbot's leave."

Albert shuddered; he had been in a trance, then, and might have awoke in the grave; the thought overpowered him, and he fainted; when he recovered himself, the two men were busily engaged, one in bathing his temples with water, and the other in endeavouring to force some wine down his throat. He eagerly demanded the water, and, though a capacious vessel, seemed as if he could have drained it to the bottom, but that Walter prevented him, and recommended a little food, which was of the coarser kind; but nature refused,—a little bread, steeped in wine, was all he could get down; and now a consultation was held as to what was the best course to be adopted, and who was to inform the baron; neither of the men liking the office, Albert besought them to conduct him beyond the castle precincts, and let it be still considered that he was dead, as his coffin could be laid in the grave in the same secret manner as though he did indeed tenant it, offering at the same time a purse containing a slight sum, his whole store of wealth, to back his suit. For some time they deliberated, but Albert assuring them that he should directly leave England, as no chance existed of the baron ever suffering him to continue in the castle, they at length consented, sooner than meet the baron's anger and the vengeance of Arnold, who was now possessed of power, and would be certain to revenge himself on them in some way for exposing his villany, since it was he who came and put the key in the door and then went back again. He had purposely left Albert to perish; and on the sixth day, having entered with Stephen and finding his captive motionless, concluded that his end was accomplished; he hastened to the baron and informed him of the death of Albert, occasioned by his obstinate abstinence, setting forth his own attention to him in a most brotherly point of light.

Fitzormond felt a pang at hearing of the death of his favourite page, when he thought of his dying uncle's injunction. He sent to the Abbot of St. Mark, who was a near relative, to request that the funeral rites might be performed as secretly as possible on the body of a serf, whom he wished laid in consecrated ground.

Jocelin, the abbot, who dreamt not of its being Albert Durand, who had ever been a favourite of his, and whom he had himself instructed in clerkly knowledge, —Albert having been an incense boy in the chapel, and ever most deferential in his manner and behaviour to the abbot and holy fathers,—Jocelin acceded to his cousin's request. And, satisfied that Sabina was now safe, the conclusion of the affair was left to Arnold, who was now promoted to all Albert's vacant offices. The heartless villain, not daring to look upon the corse of the man whose death he caused, sent Walter and Stephen to bury the body in the monks' ground, which led to the result already known. In an hour afterwards, they wrapped a cloak round Albert, and taking him through a private portal, they led him beyond the castle bounds, then refusing the purse he offered them, bid him God speed, and returned to Richborough, to proceed with the mock funeral.

When left to himself, Albert sat down on a bank at the road-side, for his weak state forbade his proceeding at a speedy rate. He looked back—it was the light dawn of a summer morn—Richborough was still to be seen, high-towering above the foggy mist, and the spires of Stonar began to sparkle in the gleam of the coming sun. Albert gazed on them, then thought of his present condition—a friendless youth thrown on a world he was ignorant of, and then going, he knew not whither, without money or means, and even denied existence, since, if known to live, his life might be the forfeit. Then would his thoughts wander to the ever absorbing object—Sabina; here reflection became too painful. He turned his eyes from the castle, and a tear trickled down his cheek; but it must be remembered he was a youth scarce eighteen, ever reared in kindness and comfort, and now driven forth to wander through an unfeeling world; by those who have ever experienced a similar outset in their juvenile days, the weakness will be forgiven, and the tear should be preserved, as one of Nature's choicest pearls.

Refreshing himself from a small flask of wine, left him by his deliverers, he proceeded, taking the route to Canterbury; but slow and feeble was his pace. Several peasants, as they met him on their way to their duties, doffed their caps as they passed, yet seemed to marvel to see so smart a youth on foot; nor it was not till Albert had proceeded some miles, that he recollected the armorial badge which he wore, in reference to his grade, and which had procured him the respect of the surrounding peasantry. He was on the point of tearing it off in an agony, for fear of being recognized, when he was overtaken by a man on horseback, who called repeatedly to him : weak as he was, fear added speed to his feet, and he hastened on, but was soon overtaken by the peasant, whom he knew as one Maurice Perkins, a good-natured, talkative fellow, and he would have fain have been without him.

"What, Master Albert," cried Maurice, "a goodly morrow to you. I spied you as you passed the miller's corner; but I would not have it it was you, the baron's favourite page, and most privileged of the whole household, going to Canterbury without a nag."

Albert gave an evasive answer to this; when the other added,—

" I know thou be'est going to Canterbury, to see the king's troops march through to-day for Dover and Calais. Well, it's but natur' that young folks should like to see such sights; and I warrant me that cross-grained chap, Mark Brandling, has denied thee thy favourite poney, as he's horse-keeper now—that be it, I know it—and thee hast taken French leave. Well, well, you be high in my lord's favour, and you will ha' your revenge against Mark Brandling, and some more on 'em; there's that Arnold Mosely, he be no better than a bad one, and I've heard him call thee, many a time; but you'll top 'em all yet. It be in thy power to do a man a good turn often, wi' my lord, and thee sha'n't want a nag to take thee to Canterbury; take this—I be only going to St. Genevieve, and there be a gay set from the castle behind, if you set spur you'll beat 'em yet. I always put up at the Swan; besides, you'll be whoam agin afore I want 'un."

Maurice had by this time got off the horse, and pressed our hero so closely to mount, that the fear of the gay set behind him, and his present weak state conjoined, Albert was induced to accept his offer. Mounting the animal, therefore, and thanking Maurice, he set off at full speed, and arrived at Canterbury without further question or molestation.

He immediately rode up to the Swan, where he found the horse was known; so, requesting the horse-keeper to take care of the animal till the owner came for it, he made his way to the public market-place, and to the cathedral-yard, where the men-at-arms were drawn up. The greater portion of the army had marched for Dover, and the rest were evacuating the city as quickly as their muster could be completed. Some light armed soldiers passing, he entered into casual conversation with them, and understanding from them that Sir Thomas Wharton was their captain, he sought that officer out, who immediately enrolled him, and promised to make him his ancient, if his prowess corresponded with his personal appearance. Calling a subordinate officer up, he entrusted Albert to him, and immediately joined a gay knot of cavaliers that were admiring the palace of the archbishop, at that time tenanted by the famous A'Beeket. A banner and light cuirass being provided for the young man, the appointments of a foot soldier of those days were soon completed; a light pike was given him, and Albert fell into the ranks.

It would have better pleased him to have served in a crossbow legion; but he was content thus to have some bias for his conduct. He saw several faces he knew well—inhabitants of Stonar and Sandwich—in the crowd, and could not refrain from a smile, as, passing through St. Augustin's-gate, two Stonar youths, clinging to the iron work, exclaimed one to the other as the light companies passed,— "Certes, if that pikeman ain't the very counterpart of Albert Durand of Richborough !"

"Poh !" says the other, " he doesn't favour him a bit. He's too tall; and see the difference a trifling change of apparel will make in some eyes."

In those days bad were the best roads; and the late rains had sadly broken up that towards Dover; they did not reach it till the afternoon following. Passing the night that intervened in a large barn, which contained his company and another, as they marched again by day-break, their sleep was but brief. No food was to be got, through bad regulations, and a drink of water was all the refreshment that could be procured, and that with considerable difficulty—two or three hundred men all at the draw-well, striving to get first served. As Albert had still a little of his wine and provisions, he had fared better than his comrades; still he felt weak, and when they arrived at Dover, he could scarcely stand.

Here again it was manifest how badly affairs were regulated, there not being shipping ready to receive the men, yet the whole army amounted to no more than 15,000. While they remained in rank, a number of nobles and superior officers rode before the line backwards and forward, joined by others who came to wish them farewell; a voice struck Albert's ear as familiar to him, and looking up, within a few paces of him, talking to a chief of division, was Baron Fitzormond on horseback, with several retainers attending, and the hated Arnold Mosely as equerry. Albert started and turned pale, and scarce could restrain himself from plunging his pike in the side of the treacherous Arnold.

The division to which Sir Thomas's company belonged was now ordered off to Walmer to embark, but were halted at Dover, and billeted on the different farms and villages around. The party to which Albert was particularly attached was at a hostel, directly on the Walmer road, just without Dover. He was seated at the door, with several of his comrades lying and lounging around, just at sun-set, when a gay troop rode up, and again, to his no small discomforture, he recognised the attendants of Fitzormond, several of whom dismounted and entered the hostel, though merely the result of accident, that being their route home. Albert could not conceive but that they came after him, and while his comrades were engaged in conversation with the new comers, Albert made his way into the fields, and struck into a wood that extended for some miles; nor till he had travelled to some distance did he consider that he was deserting from the royal army with his accoutrements. To return now was too late, as his absence must have been noted, and he would be blamed and doubtless punished, as instances of desertion had been frequent.

As Albert approached the coast, not knowing what to do, he pursued the track he was in till he came out into the road which leads to Deal and Stonar: unacquainted with the locality, he mechanically took the right-hand turn, and walked at a brisk rate, fearing to fall in with any of the parties billeted on the surrounding hamlet. While thus buried in thought, the sound of horses' hoofs struck on his ear. Screening himself under the shade of an overspeading oak, he waited till the horseman should have passed. It was a bright moonlight night, and he could plainly distinguish it was but a single rider. Just as he came opposite to the tree behind which Albert stood, the horse stumbled, which, taking his rider by surprise, he was fairly thrown out of the stirrups on the road. A curse and exclamation revealed him to be Arnold Mosely. Albert could restrain himself no longer. The pike he had left at his quarters, but drawing his sword, and springing into the road, he stood before the astonished equerry. Never was terror and astonishment depicted in the countenance more fearfully vivid than in the face of the startled Arnold.

" Does the grave give up its dead ?" he hoarsely muttered.

" To punish thy falsity, accursed villain !" cried Albert. " Draw, coward, and defend thy life !" at the same time making a pass at him.

Mechanically did the other draw his sword, and parry the thrust of his enraged adversary. It was evident his whole frame was paralyzed, and he took but little care to defend himself. In a minute after he fell weltering in his blood ; a home lunge of Albert's had driven the sword clean through his body, and its point came out just beneath the right shoulder. A deep groan bespoke the fatal nature of the wound. When Albert came up to him he was insensible ; his face was deadly pale, and his teeth immoveably clenched. He lay on his back in a pool of blood. The circumstances admitted no time for delay ; Albert snatched up the cloak that had fallen from the shoulders of Mosely, and seizing the bridle of the horse, who was quietly browsing near the spot, he mounted it. Base as the conduct of the man had been, Albert could not but feel a sensation of regret as he gazed on the form of him who had been his bosom friend.

Turning the horse's head from the coast, he set off at full speed, to go he knew not whither. As he rode on, he bethought him of the slender stock of money he possessed, for the little sum the purse contained had been mostly expended at Canterbury, and on the march ; and nothing could have induced him to have rifled the person of Arnold, though he made no doubt he carried money, which the next comer would appropriate to his own use. He never drew his rein till the short breathings of the animal he rode on gave warning of the miles he had travelled, and the jaded state it was in.

He had now reached what was then called, and is to the present day, styled the Weald of Kent, a particularly wild and barren spot, where, in late years, has been found a Roman galley, embedded in the soil, a proof that the sea had made great inroads formerly, and since retired.

Albert, dismounting from his tired steed, removed the bridle, and suffered the weary animal to graze—a stream of water that crossed the road, being welcome to both man and beast. He then stretched himself on the roots of an ancient elm, and meditated on the late events, wondering what fate had next in store for him, his late adventures being none of the most common kind. He had been revenged on his enemy—but that revenge, beyond the gratification, had been of no service. He blamed himself for being too hasty. He should have forced the villain at the sword's point into the presence of the baron, and made him confess. Still that would not have satisfied the father, and his affair with Sabina would still have excluded him from the castle. While thus employed, sleep overcame him, and in his dream he was welcomed back to the castle, his offence forgiven, and Sabina kind as ever. A command was obtained for him, and a promise made that Sabina's hand should reward his prowess.

From this delightful vision he was awoke by the sound of loud voices, and looking up, he found himself surrounded by a party of ten or a dozen men of ferocious appearance, armed to the teeth. At first his idea was, that they were the soldiers in pursuit of him, but a second glance convinced him that their appointments were not military, nor was their appearance soldier-like. One of them broke silence by saying,—

" Hilloa, comrade ! who gave you permission to quarter yourself and horse on these lands ? You belong to the royal army by the mounting of your arms—a runaway trooper I take—taken the king's money, and decamped with it. You must allow us to play the same game with you."

Albert now saw that he had fallen into the hands of freebooters. Rising from the ground, he said,—

" My friends, however near your remark may be to the truth in the foregoing part of your observation, I can assure you that the latter portion of it is without foundation. I have not received the king's money, and to prove it, I have but this trifle about me, which I am ashamed to present you. My horse and arms are my only wealth."

The men looked at each other, and then seemed to confer with one another. The first speaker then turning to Albert, said,—

" Whither go you ?"

To which our hero immediately answered,—

" That he knew not. All the world was alike to him. He had been spurned from the home of his childhood—had been a villain's victim, whom, in revenge, he had slain, which had caused his expulsion from the army. He now wandered he knew not where. He was a marked and injured man—life but a barren moor, choked up by the thorny brambles of penury and woe. Do what you will," added he, " I care not, for I am fortune's toy—a feather in the gale of fate, for ever tempest-tossed."

" Wouldst thou become a freeman ?" asked three in the same breath.

" I would," was the reply.

" Can you be faithful ?"

" The trial will prove."

" Can you be secret ?"

" As the grave."

At the end of this colloquy, the principal robber, after some conference, told Albert to follow. At the same time another of the band bound his eyes with a scarf, and he was then hurried back into the forest. His guards continued silent, but he could distinguish that they had drawn their swords. Also he could hear the welcome sound of his horse's hoofs, and the jingle of his accoutrements warned him that they were descending into a hollow place. That it was roofed, he was certain, by the reverberation. At last they paused, and Albert felt himself hurried forward a dozen paces, and the bandage being removed from his eyes, he found himself in a large vaulted apartment, similar that of the abbot's, in St. Mark's Monastery, as he thought, only larger, and less ornamented. A couch stood at the farther end, on which lay a young man, of imposing address and winning appearance. His dress was of costly material, and cunningly put together, but stained and despoiled by riot and debauchery. There was a restless ferocity in his eye that was a contradiction to the bland smile that played round his mouth.

" What have you there, Rufus ?" said he, as Albert and his guards advanced.

" A new hand, noble captain, if it please ye," answered the robber ; " one that has left the army, because he liked best to sleep in a whole skin."

" Cowards hive not with us, drone," said the captain, frowning on the speaker, who seemed taken aback by the remark.

" I am no coward, captain," said Albert, with hauteur ; " but I care not to return to certain disgrace and punishment. Add to which, not five hours since I slew my enemy, and that is in itself enough to seal my fate. Yet I fear not death. A brave man may dread punishment."

" Right ; give me your hand, Saxon," said the captain, rising from his seat. " Your speech convinces me you are brave man. Welcome, brother—you shall be enrolled a Free Ranger."

With that, he threw open the door near him, and seizing Albert's hand, they entered a long vaulted apartment, exceeding the other in dimensions. A table was placed the whole length of the room, with an antique chair raised near three feet above the rest, at the head, for the captain, and a similar one raised about two feet, at the bottom, for the lieutenant, or second in command, who was seated with above fifty of the band, when Albert and the captain entered. The latter was received with great respect and cheering, all rising bareheaded. He took his place, and seating Albert on his right hand, after a slight pause, addressed the society, which considerably augmented, after the entrance of the chief. " Free Rangers," exclaimed the chief, " I introduce you a new brother, whom I deem worthy of a place in our community."

A general shout followed this. The captain added,—

" He is one whose steel has tasted blood ere now."

Albert here drew his sword, which was crimsoned with gore, having no time, when he drew it forth from Arnold's body, to wipe or cleanse it. This action, and the accompanying observation, was received witn shouts again. " Fill all," cried the captain, pouring out from a silver ewer, into two goblets of the same metal, a stream of rosy wine to the brim of each vessel, an example immediately followed by the band.

" Your name ?" turning to Albert. Albert hesitated. He was but humbly born; but his ancestors had been honest, and his name had stood fair in men's mouths. He, therefore, resolved to use a fictitious name here, as he had before done when enrolled in Sir Thomas's company, a precaution he had since applauded himself for. He answered, boldly, therefore, Adrian de Morven.

"A health to our new brother, Adrian," said the captain, finishing at a draught his ample portion, the lieutenant and band copying their leader with religious exactness. "Now, Adrian, listen," continued the chief, "the rules of the Free Rangers are strict and binding. The man that turns craven is dismissed the band. If he lives to reach the extremity of the forest we have no objection to his settling where he pleases."

Albert shuddered at the derisive laugh that gave notice that the poor wretch would be surely murdered to prevent his revealing what he had seen and participated in.

"We have wholesome laws, too, the first of which is, that all plunder, gold or gear, alive or dead, is the general property, nothing being exclusively an individual's right, but by the general consent of the band. We are all bound to revenge a brother's wrongs. The interests of the band take precedence of all other duty or feeling. Parent, brother, wife, or child, or friend, a Free Ranger is bound to sacrifice, if the interests of the community require it."

A cold tremor ran through his frame as Albert listened to the sanguinary code.

"You are bound at all times and all hazards to obey the command of your captain, who is elected from the band by ballot, or general acclaim. The lieutenant to be chosen by the chief, who is to be obeyed in the same manner as the captain, except where the orders are in opposition to his commands. If any of the Free Rangers shall fall into captivity, he may be assured that the band will set him free if it is possible; but it will surely find a way to be revenged upon him if he reveal aught of the secrets of the band, which are to hold together till it shall be dissolved by general consent. The services of a Free Ranger can cease only with his life; he can never marry. Any dispute occurring about a female, the captain's claim supersedes, or the lieutenant is bound to destroy her to prevent ill blood in the community. All children brought into the cavern to be slain, the lieutenant losing his appointment if any child escape unscathed. A Free Ranger allowed leave of absence, his bond being taken for his return, signed with his blood; if he forfeit, he surely dies. These rules you swear to abide by, and to see fulfilled."

The band all drew their swords. The rules, written in fair characters, and signed by the two chiefs with their blood, lay on the table, and all crossing their swords over it, Albert's being uppermost, all exclaimed with a loud voice,—

"We swear."

After which Albert had individually to repeat,—

"I swear."

Then all filled their goblets, and holding the wine in the left hand, and the sword drawn in the right, the captain gave,—

"Disgrace and death in this world, and eternal torment in the next, to the Free Ranger that breaks his bond."

The toast was repeated by all, and the wine drank—this ceremony was always repeated on the reception of a new member; the lieutenant then rising, said,—

"To imprint the importance of the oath he has taken more firmly on the memory, let the new brother follow—'Council of Death,' attend."

Twelve rangers then rose from their seats and went out through a small portal in the side of the chamber, followed by Albert and the lieutenant. After passing through several passages, they came to the Hall of Justice, as it was designated—the Hall of Torture had been a more fitting appellation. It was a large chamber, painted black; everything belonging or appertaining to it, was of the same sombre hue. A kind of throne was raised in it for the chief; and immediately before it—in the way of a modern clerk's desk—one for the lieutenant. On one side were two rows of benches for the Council of Death; on the opposite side a large, clumsy-looking chair for the prisoner. This chair, as he was shown, by a spring being

See page 24.

touched, could seize or hold the wretched being so that he could not move either hand or foot. Around the hall were instruments of torture—the boot, the thumb-screw, pincers, &c., at the end was the rack. One-half of the place was taken up by rows of benches opposite the throne, and commanding a view of the proceedings, for the use of the general band. The place was well calculated to inspire fear.

Passing through a portal in the side of this apartment, they came to a range of dungeons; the lieutenant taking a key from his girdle unlocked one of them, which, on entering, was found to contain a prisoner, the most wretched object human eye e'er gazed upon—a few rags alone covered him. His hair and beard were matted, and so far exceeding customary limits, that he looked more like some wild beast than a human being. What could be seen of the face was pallor'd o'er with the stone-coloured sickly hue of death. His eyes were sunk so deep in the sockets, that it was only when the gleam of the lights they carried with them flashed upon them they could be seen. Every limb was broken, and the flesh of his legs and arms torn by pincers and bleeding. An iron girdle went round his waist, and a collar of the same kind round his neck, and a similar one round his left ancle; from each of these was suspended a heavy chain, the end of which was fastened to a ring in the floor—a needless precaution, since it was impossible the poor wretch could stand, or even move. In the intense and incessant agony he suffered, he could not help but groan continually. He had been racked the afternoon previous; all his cry was for water, a jug of which stood near him. He could not lift it with his hand, and was obliged to extend his head and drink out of it as it stood on the ground, consequently it was soon reduced beyond the mark that he could reach to; and it was piteous to behold his attempt to dip his fingers into the jug, with the arm broke in two places—one above and the other beneath the elbow. To one of the council, who lifted the jug to his lips, the lieutenant spoke rather sharply.

"Do you," he cried, "a free ranger, and a member of the death council, do you show kindness to one who has forfeited his bond, and betrayed the band? Let him howl and die in misery! Adieu!" he sternly cried, as he locked the door, and left the wretch to perish. "Adieu! You see the punishment of the perjured!"

Albert's flesh seemed to creep upon his bones. To the last hour did the look of that poor dying wretch seem to stand in his mind's eye. On their return to the place of carousel, they drank deep, and passed the greater part of the night, when he was shown to a dormitory, where each had a humble couch.

As Albert extended himself on his, he could not help deeply reflecting on the late bustling events of his life. Each new change seemed for the worse; he could not but feel that he was now a degraded being, despite the military air thrown upon the proceedings of the band. He was a thief—a common foot-pad, linked to a body of bad men by a wicked vow, which certainly must call down the vengeance of man, and the justice of Heaven.

How different was his situation but a few days since. In the army he might have risen to honours and wealth; that course now was hopeless; he was a man marked and proscribed; his existence, calculating on the chances of a robber's life, but brief, and his position in society, humble as it had been, he must never hope to attain again. Heart-worn and chafed in mind, the wine he had drunk had failed to exhilarate him—he sat in the cavern a pitiable object—a sober being, amongst drunken men; but he had been able to note how hollow the joys of debauchery are—a life of horror! seldom or ever to see the light of day! but cower amid caverns and glooms, suffered to breathe the air only when engaged in a fray, or work of spoliation!

The brief period of rest beneath the tree where the robbers found him, had been his chief repose since he left the castle. It was long ere sleep relieved his care-worn mind. How long he had slept he knew not, when he was roughly awoke by Rufus, who, giving him a hearty shake, asked him if he was going to sleep for ever. Hastily rising, and rubbing his eyes, Albert demanded to know the time, and if it was morning.

"It was that ere we retired," said Rufus. "You have slept till nearly night-fall. You forget that here night is day, and day is night. The curfew is our chanticleer."

Albert sighed as he thought of the pleasant world that he had left behind, and following Rufus, he entered into what might be termed the robbers' kitchen, where a plentiful repast of venison (fresh) and beer awaited him. It must be remembered that such was the breakfast of the first of the land in those days, when tea, and coffee, and such like, were unknown. The beer, too, at that time was a very different beverage to that known by the same name now-a-days. Having despatched his meal, Rufus showed him the armory, a place well supplied with arms of all kinds, and all nations, amongst which was a curious glass dagger. The manufacture of glass was then unknown in England, and almost exclusively enjoyed by the Venetians. The weapon in question came from there, though apparently more for show, as a toy. It was a deadly weapon, though not brought into general use till some generations afterwards, mankind revolting at its horrible effect. Any person being stabbed with it, the force of the blow broke off the blade, and it remained in the flesh, stopping the passage of the blood and the skin closing over it. No wound was perceptible to the unsuspecting observer. In after ages, when the use of this diabolical weapon became frequent in the hands of the Italian bravoes, a handle of metal was so contrived, that a glass blade could be fixed to them, in a manner something similar to the steel pens of modern days, to their holders, so that the same handle served for a number of blades. In the present instance it was almost the infancy of the art. The whole of it was composed of glass, of a white, coarse kind. This weapon particularly engaged Albert's attention, probably from its substance, as at that early period glass was but little used in England, that only of the coarsest kind, for windows, and those not general. The horse armory, too, was very complete, and curious of its kind.

They next went to the stables, which contained stalls or holding, for a hundred steeds ; the major part of the band being out on a forage, but few of the animals were left, but Albert, who was an admirable judge of horse-flesh, was taken with the appearance of the creatures, all of which were of the best breed and mettle, and for beauty and condition might vie with the stud of the proudest noble, or military horse legion. His own, or rather Arnold's mare, was there, but bore marks of great distress, and in all points suffered, by a comparison with the horses of the band. Several of the band were busy in attending to their chargers, and others employed in cleaning arms. On his going into the chamber where he had sat the previous night, he found all things prepared for the return of the band. The viands were in process of cooking ; no less then eight men being engaged in the culinary duties, it requiring no small quantity of food for so large a number, each of whom seemed blessed with an appetite that might have astonished a modern alderman. Three sheep, and a proportionate quantity of venison, and hog's-flesh, being roasted and boiled for the ensuing meal, which, though it might have puzzled a gourmand of the present day to have decided which it should be termed, supper, or dinner, was the principal meal of the robbers, who only took that, and a breakfast of cold meat, &c., two meals being considered in those days, and by such societies, as sufficient, and every person who had seen the quantity consumed by each individual, would have acquiesced in the belief of its sufficiency. Filling a goblet from the ample vessels of drink that graced the board, Rufus pledged his new comrade, and proceeded to give him an account of his new associates.

"Our captain," said the robber, "is a younger brother of a noble house, and would have been compelled to become a monk, but for the line of life he had struck into ; the name he goes by in the band is Bertrand Bayard. He is a fine spirited fellow, but rather strict in his discipline, and never known to forgive the slightest injury, or even jest at his expence. It is impossible to know when you have him, for he will address a man in the kindest manner, and yet in less than an hour after condemn him to punishment. But he is mildness itself compared to the lieutenant, Fransisco Vicard, of Italian extraction, and originally a butcher of Winchester, where his ancestors had followed the trade for some years. His practice in killing calves and oxen had given him a taste for blood in general, till he turned human butcher, and few had ever slain more of his fellow creatures with his own hands than Fransisco Vicard. He seems to take a delight in the sufferings of the human frame, and has been known to hang half-a-dozen victims that had fallen into the hands of the banditti, while he sat and drank, and enjoyed the sight."

With any of the band who had attempted to leave, or had otherwise violated the rules, he was dreadfully severe ; the poor wretch whom Albert had seen was one who had purloined a quantity of gold, and taking one of the best horses ha attempted to make his way to the north, to the place of his nativity; he had been overtaken, and condemned by the band to be given over to the council of death, which was composed, as before stated, of twelve men chosen from the band, and filled up according as they were taken off by death, or choosing to resign, which any of them might do after a year's service, being only bound to hold their commission for twelve months. A prisoner being found guilty by the general voice of the band, was given over by the captain to the council of death, at the head of which the lieutenant, as the thirteenth or casting vote, was perpetual foreman; the nature of his punishment, and the style and quantity of torture, was decided by this council—the majority overruling the other; the foreman, or lieutenant, in the first place, giving his opinion, which in general decided the rest, though sometimes stormy discussions arise, and the sense of the majority is then taken and abided by, even if against the opinion of the foreman. This, in some degree, resembled the jury of the present times; but, as it may be supposed, the opinion of the chief generally prevailing. As may be also imagined the character of the lieutenant gave the colour to the punishments; if he was of a sanguinary turn, they were dreadful; if he was lenient, so were they.

It has been already observed, that Fransisco delighted in torture and scenes of blood; he was brave to a fault, and, had he been a soldier, would have been a worthy example of patience under hardship and deprivation, and unflinching adherence to duty and discipline; as it was, he was hated by the band for his severity, and though he looked to be made captain if aught happened to the chief, it was generally supposed that he would be opposed by the majority of the rangers. The captain himself was not in much better odour with them; but he was generous, and at times liberal and merciful, and his capacity and fitness for his office none disputed, but his hypocrisy was proverbial, and, as Rufus observed, it was impossible to know, in common parlance, "when you had him." Of the band individually it was impossible to speak, they were men of all grades and many nations, all desperate characters, and little could be said, as may be judged, of either their morals or their hearts. "For my own part," added Rufus, "I am the son of a freeman, who had but two children, me and my brother; each of us tried to undermine the other; for no two brothers could be more unlike in their hearts and pursuits; yet, I'll take Heaven to witness, I never tried to injure him, till I had detected Allan forming plans for my undoing. Nature's law is retaliation, and that law I followed; yet, notwithstanding, his superior cunning prevailed, and my father bequeathed all to him. We were twins; and care had not been taken at our birth to ascertain which of us came into the world first; my mother, with her dying breath, declared it was me, but my brother contrived to bribe a woman who had officiated as nurse to swear that he came into the world first; I was left wholly dependent on him, and he treated me as the veriest serf; my temper rose against it, I resisted his tyranny, and he struck me. Revenge for the base trick he had played me smothered all fraternal feeling, and I buried my dagger in his side.

"Richmond was no place for me then, and I fled; so that neither benefitted by the possessions, and to whom they went I know not. There was a host of relatives, and I left them to fight it out among themselves. I wandered into this part of the country, and was found in a similar state to that in which I discovered you, and became one of the band. I am now what is termed sub-lieutenant, or third officer, holding command in the cave when the other two are out, but having no higher voice or power than the rest in the general muster.

"Sentries are placed in the cavern, and outposts in the wood and places adjoining, so that it is next to an impossibility that any one can escape—bribery being here of no avail; and when on a foray, a suspected party is so closely watched that the least treacherous movement would cost him his life.

"You now know the character of the society you belong to. A band so formidable, that even justice is afraid to tackle them. Some day we shall become so notorious that troops will be sent to put us down; rewards, and the presence of a protecting power, will induce the peasants to betray our hiding-place.

Much blood spilt, and many lives lost, will he the result; and the remainder of the band will be hung up on the forest trees like dogs. Such will be the ultimate fate of the Free Rangers. So come, drink, and enjoy life as long as you can. I like you, and will be your friend. Do your duty boldly and fearlessly, and you'll yet make more friends. In a society like this you can't have too many."

Albert thanked the robber for his kindness and information, and committed all that he had said carefully to memory.

'Tis useless to dwell on the routine of a robber's life, confined as Albert was; suffice to say, that after having been kept almost as a prisoner in the cavern for a length of time, he was one day informed by the captain that his term of probation had expired, and that evening he was to make one of a scouting party, under the command of Fransisco, the lieutenant. Much as Albert longed to breathe the free air again, he sickened at the idea of being concerned in a predatory excursion, particularly in company with the lieutenant, who seemed to have taken a singular dislike to him, and never failed to insult and deride him whenever it lay in his power. But for the captain, who kept to the word he originally pledged to him, his life would have been insupportable. But, remembering what Rufus had told him, and knowing from every day experience that silent obedience was rigorously exacted, he prepared himself for the occasion, taking care to alter his original appearance as much as possible.

Fourteen men, besides himself and the lieutenant, being now mustered in the stable, they took their horses (one of which was allotted to each man, who had the sole care of the animal, any omission in the duties of which, as well as in the cleaning and order of his arms, was punished with as much rigour as in a royal regiment), and led them in single file to the entrance, which was a small portal amid the ruins of an old castle or fortress. This entrance was so low that the men were obliged to stoop, and the horses, kneeling down, fairly walked on their knees through, dropping on their haunches as they rose upon their fore legs, their knees being protected by strong leather caps for the purpose. They then mounted, and struck through the forest. Though the shades of night had closely gathered around, the air was exceedingly grateful to Albert after confinement.

The strictest silence was preserved, and after riding some few miles, they halted at a place where several roads or tracks joined, roads at that time of day being hardly worthy of the name. Here they were drawn up, two deep, and ordered to remain in silence till they should hear the signal. Having issued this command, the lieutenant rode leisurely on till a turning in the wood hid him from their view. The men then broke silence, and began talking to each other.

" What is this object of the lieutenant's to-night?" asked one.

" He's after some booty that Black Robert, the spy, brought notice of this morning. We are likely to have a smart brush of it, too."

On this, all eyes were turned on the speaker, who was asked to] tell all he knew about it.

" I only know," he answered, " that some treasure is on its way to London, guarded by an escort of soldiers, and we are to attack it."

" What is the number of them?" asked the first speaker. " I don't like having anything to do with the soldiers."

" Only six, and their officer," was the reply, when a low whistle was heard.

The leading couple now turned their horses' heads in the direction of the sound, and, followed by the rest, rode off in an easy canter. They were soon met by the lieutenant, who bid them pause and listen. The sound of horses' hoofs were plainly to be heard, and the heavy jingle of arms against armour.

" Lieutenant," said the one who had been telling the band of the coming party, and who had dismounted, to lay his ear to the ground, " there are more of them than you bargained for. I'll swear to there being more than a dozen horses at least. We shall have our hands full."

" Fool," said the lieutenant, " what you mistake for so many horses, are the sumpter mules, laden with the treasure. The force does not exceed half a dozen armed men."

"The arms of half a dozen wouldn't make that cursed noise," doggedly answered the man. "I know what I hear."

"Cowards sometimes hear double," sarcastically said the lieutenant; "but whatever you hear, have the kindness to keep silence, or look to the consequences. Forward." With this threat the lieutenant put his horse in motion, followed by the rest, till an opening in the thick brushwood exposed a part of the main road.

"Halt!" said the lieutenant; "draw, and be ready to attack at the word."

He was obeyed, and every eye was fixed on the opening. At length two men riding in advance, *en militaire*, were seen to pass. In a minute after, the main party, three abreast, the sumpter horse, or mule, between, began to show themselves, when the word was given, and the robbers made a furious charge; but as Albert emerged from the wood, the sight that met his eye made him check his horse's speed. Down the road, as far as the eye could distinguish in the gloom, was a line of horsemen, three and four deep, making force of at least not less than forty armed men, clad in armour, with the royal badge upon their cloaks. They in turn made as firm an attack upon the robbers. The *melee* was fierce and tremendous; the horses of the robbers reeled against the weight of the opposing chargers, who, like their riders, were covered with plates of mail. It was four to one, and a decided superiority of arms. The robbers fell fast under the tremendous blows of the soldiers' battle-axes, striking them front and back at the same moment. Albert received a blow, that nearly severed his basnett in two, and he was obliged to fight like a tiger, to hew himself a passage.

The lieutenant, seeing that all was hopeless, in a loud voice gave the word to "Retreat to the rendezvous," which was a large tree, about three miles from the spot, and one from the cavern, which he had pointed out as they passed, ordering them, if separated, to make to it, previous to mustering for their return, a course which prevented any pursuit betraying the cave. With much difficulty, and many wounds, eight of the band, including Albert and the lieutenant, made their way into the forest, taking separate routes, pursued by the infuriated soldiery, the rest of the banditti being literally cut to pieces; and had not those who did escape had their horses' heads armed with spiked frontlets, it would have been impossible for them to have made their way out of the throng, the physical force of their antagonists being so overpowering. Albert was pursued by three horsemen, and was weak and bleeding from the wound he had received on his head, and another on his left arm. Close pressed, he plunged into the thickest part of the wood, slashing away the brushwood and branches, to clear the passage for his horse, who, used to the kind of chase, plunged through, and aided him by forcing his way by his weight. In this, however, he frequently had to exchange cuts with his enemies, but two of which now kept up with him, one of whom, with his whole collected force, cut at Albert, with a heavy two-handed sword, a severe back stroke. Fortunately for him, an overhanging branch partly warded off the blow, but the point cut through his leather surcoat just above his breast-plate, and sunk into his shoulder, nearly depriving him entirely of the use of his sword arm. One of the soldier's horses now stumbled, and severely threw his rider. The other kept up with Albert but a minute or two after, and believing from the appearance of the blood, for he was now covered with gore, that he soon must drop, slackened the speed of his horse, and turned back to assist his comrade.

Albert now trusted to his horse's sagacity, for the left arm being also wounded, he could scarcely hold the rein, much less guide him. He knew not whereabouts he was in the forest, but the tree had been the accustomed rendezvous, and the animal made his own way to it as soon as they cleared the brushwood. Albert there found the lieutenant and four more attending to a sixth, that had fallen from his steed from loss of blood. His wounds were dreadful and numerous, and in a few minutes he died, with bitter execrations on his lips. The scene was horrible: both men and horses were literally drenched in blood. Another joined soon after Albert, and then, after waiting a short time, and being convinced, from what each had seen, that they had collected all that could be mustered, they placed the dead ranger across his steed, and another taking the bridle, they set off for the cavern, where, after the lieutenant had sounded his horn, and the sign and countersign had been exchanged, the door was opened, and the wounded party admitted. The captain and a great part of the band received them at the stables, and roughly sympathised with them for their defeat, bemoaning the death of their companions, and bitterly cursing the soldiery, whom they swore to be revenged upon. The robber who had warned the lieutenant previous to the attack, now openly accused him of gross negligence and want of care in not reconnoitring, thereby losing one half of their number. This opinion was confirmed by the captain and the whole band. Fransisco, though swelling with indignation, could only cast looks of vengeance on his accuser, and load the name of Black Robert with execrations.

The high encomiums passed on Albert, to whose determined bravery in cutting a passage through his steeled opponents they ascribed the means of the remnant being preserved, also stung the lieutenant to the quick. Their wounds were now examined, there being no less than three experienced and clever men, that served as leeches in the band, two of whom but seldom quitted the cavern, which suited them well, one being fond of a life of ease and enjoyment of the table, and the other was not over fond of fighting. A third, however, was a brave man, and always made one of the party in the captain's forays.

The wounds of Albert were considered as dangerous, particularly that which had cut through the morion, or basnett, a part of which was driven into his head, fortunately in the front, or the brain had been injured. During the process he fainted, and the band, with whom he was beginning to be a great favourite, were alarmed. The gash on his shoulder was frightful, and he had a wound in the left thigh, as well as arm. They bore high testimony of his courage, and capability of receiving as well as giving. With a very different eye they looked upon their lieutenant's wounds, which were both behind; and though he really was brave to a fault, yet they made severe remarks upon the contrast between him and Albert, to whom, from that hour, he bore a deadly hatred.

CHAPTER II.

MORE than a month had elapsed ere Albert, or Adrian, as he was now called, had recovered from his wounds, and consequently could attend to his duties. About this time, a traveller with a young boy, his son, had been stopped in the forest. The father had been murdered, and the boy, whose name was Cyril Gaveston, was brought by Rufus and Jasper (the man who had so severely accused the lieutenant) to the cave. When the question was mooted as to what should be done with the boy, the captain proposed his being brought up in the cave as a future member of the band. A number of opinions were expressed, many remarking that he would always remember the fate of his father, perhaps be tempted to betray them, and be the destruction of the whole community. Though Albert in secret coincided with this opinion, as being the course he should himself take, yet he saw if he did not give his vote in favour of the captain's proposition, the boy would most probably be savagely butchered. The discussion had been carried on some time, and argument was high, when Fransisco, rising, imposed silence by striking with his partizan upon the table.

" Has it ever occurred," he said, at the same time frowning haughtily on all around—" has it ever occurred to this sapient council, that neither they, nor their leader, have any jurisdiction in this affair? By the wise code framed by the founder of this society, no child should be permitted to live. Women, priests, and children, are ever babbling, and danger must accrue from it. It is the province of the second in command to avert the danger, by ridding the cavern of the object, and slaying it, as a sacrifice on the altar of safety. I claim the boy, and, to end all disputes, my dagger shall now drink his blood. Bring the urchin hither," he added, in a voice of thunder, to two of the band, who soon brought the trembling child before his cruel executioner.

The band murmured pity, as they looked upon the fair boy; his golden ringlets falling in clusters on his shoulders, and his white tunic and ermined buskins giving him the appearance of some bright spirit, some aerial being constrained by some wicked sorcerer. Albert had made up his own mind to the affair, as it gave him an opportunity of putting a test in force, on which he much relied.

"He is but young," said the captain.

"Look to your rules. He is capable of telling a straight-forward tale; besides, 'tis my province—who dares to stay me? The boy shall die."

So saying, he rose hastily, and striding towards the youth, drew his dagger. The poor child clung instinctively to its guards, and prayed for mercy in tones so piteous, that it might have moved a heart of stone—still no one moved. Like the cat purring over its prey, Fransisco stood with folded arms, a savage smile upon his countenance, gazing on the agony of fear that manifested itself in the boy's countenance.

"What should fright the boy? Why do you fear me, pretty child?" he cried, with an insulting sneer.

"I do fear you," answered the boy; "you killed my father. None struck him but you; you are a cruel man."

Turning to the band exultingly, Fransisco cried,—

"You hear! Where are the fools that would let this babbler live?" with that, he dashed his iron gauntlet in the face of the boy, who reeled, covered with blood. The other advanced to strike him with his dagger, when Albert stepped suddenly between, and struck it out of his hand, at the same time hurling the murderer to the other end of the place. Shouts of applause followed this; the captain and all started on their legs. Hastily springing up and drawing his sword, Fransisco cried, in the hoarse guttural tones of rage and hatred,—

"Villain, at length I have drawn thee out in thy true colours. When that my arm has mastered your puny strength" (and truly he seemed a burly giant to Albert) "I will have thee condemned to every torture ingenuity can devise. Think of the hall of torture—the prison—the dungeon."

Albert shuddered with horror. The look and action were taken for craven fear, so Fransisco deemed, and, with bitter contempt curling his lip, he cried, in mock condescension,—

"Nay, poor fool, I forgive thee. Drink; the praises showered on you by a set of knaves and cowards hath made thee mad. One victim will suffice for me to-day. Kneel, and sue for pardon; kneel, I say, or, by hell, I'll have thee racked till every atom writhes with its own peculiar agony. Kneel, I say."

Albert fell on his knee before his giant antagonist; a shout of derision followed; Fransisco smiled in fiendish exultation.

"I kneel as you have bid me," said Albert; "I kneel to implore you to spare that helpless child."

"Never!" shouted Fransisco, stamping on the rocky flooring in rage. "Never, I say! He shall die as surely as I live."

"Then," cried Albert, springing up, and drawing his falchion, "here's at thee, thou tyrant accursed!"

The shouts of the gang were now deafening. Those who were immediate friends of Albert, and they comprised the major part of the auditors, drew their weapons, and formed a ring, keeping all off from interfering with the combatants. With deadly fury they engaged; their swords struck fire at every blow, till they seemed wrapt in sparks; the iron mail of Fransisco yielded to the blows of Albert, as his cut into the other's leather surcoat, for Albert, as an invalid, was out of armour—the other had a breast-plate and back-piece; both were bare-headed. A blow of the lieutenant's laid open one of Albert's late wounds, and he started back with the extreme pain; but the voice of the band cheered him on, and his sword's point caught Fransisco in the throat, giving a horrid gash. He staggered, when Albert, with a furious back-handed cut, nearly severed his head from his body; the robbers shouted as the lieutenant fell, and Albert was loaded with encomiums. The captain—who was really pleased that Fransisco, whom he always hated, was removed—seeing that Albert was so popular with the band, overlooked the rule, by which, whoever drew weapon on either chief incurred the penalty of death.

On order being re-established, and the body of the late second in command removed till ready for interment, the captain convoked the band, and decided that the boy should live. The captain then named Albert second in command, at the same time declaring that Rufus had a prior claim; but that he chose Albert, as he conceived it met the wishes of the society; this was received with three cheering shouts. Albert immediately rose and declined in favour of Rufus,

not wishing to make any one his enemy; but the latter stating that he was content, and that he conceived Albert more becoming the situation than himself, our hero was formally inducted into the command; a night of revelry and riot followed, and all went on as before. Cyril was gratitude itself, and though not suffered to quit the cavern, was kindly treated by the band in general, till his youth and lapse of time getting the better of his grief, he by degrees got reconciled to his fate; time passed, and Albert every day grew a greater favourite with the band, but ambition had tainted his mind. He coveted the sole command, and so desirous was he of the captain's power, that his whole time, day and night, was passed in devising how to compass his object; the scenes of blood and rapine he had now engaged in for years, hardened his heart, and murder became a matter unheeded.

Returning home from their forays one fine night, after the pillage of a monastery, a mile or better from the cavern, Albert and the captain dismounted, and giving their horses in charge to the men, ordered them to proceed with Rufus. A foray of danger was then on foot, and Albert would fain have dissuaded the captain, as they walked on arguing in their moonlight progress. They came to the edge of a precipice, at the foot of whose rocky side a deep pool, the remnant of waters long since retired, was so overspread by noxious weeds and tangling briar, as to deceive the eye as to whether it was land or water; but once immersed, no human power could save the luckless wight. As he gazed on its green surface, and calculated the height, he saw that here an opportunity presented itself to make him all he wished. It was a damning act; but was it the first? The unsuspecting chief looked over the edge to note what had engaged the attention of his lieutenant; the moment could not return; another might never present itself. Albert stabbed his superior in the back, and hurled him over the brink. The body struck upon the rocky points twice, then plunged into the pool; the black waters gleamed for a moment in the light of the moon, and then the duckweed covered the place as though nothing had occurred to disturb its reign, while all the loathsome inhabitants of the stagnant lake, in miniature, began their attacks on the yet warm body of the hapless chief.

As Albert moved on towards the cavern the moon seemed like a ball of blood, or crimson fire, the trees assumed demoniac shapes, and the voices of those he had murdered seemed to call him when he reached the cavern. His pale countenance and looks of alarm excited curiosity in the band. He gave an account of falling in with a party of hunters, and being compelled to strike into the wood, the captain had missed the track, and, closely pressed, had leaped down into the precipice. Some of the band suspected all was not right; but nothing could be proved, and few murmurs were heard.

Albert now succeeded to the command, and appointed Rufus his lieutenant; to Cyril he ever showed kindness. Years passed, the Albert of former years was changed to the heartless robber now, whose dreams were terrific, whose guilty soul knew no peace, and who indulged in sensual pleasures to drive away reflection. His darling project ever presented itself to his mind, to invest Richborough castle at night, effect an entrance and murder all, all but her who alone had power over his withered heart; but all weighty projects must be laid before the society; he feared their proposal. It was well known that Richborough castle could last a long siege, and was bravely defended. He trusted to taking it by surprise; they were not so sanguine; and what availed it?—Sabina had forgotten him. Seven years had passed since then; what hope had he, a proscribed man, the captain of a banditti? None—none!

While sitting in his chamber, ostensibly auditing the accounts of the band, after the fashion of figures then, but, in truth, racking himself with the recollections of the past, Jasper came in, to inform him that some prisoners had been taken, and a goodly sum.

Albert gave a listless answer, and was proceeding with his former occupation, when the robber asked what was to be done with the lady.

"What lady?"

"That which was brought in but now—she and her father, seemingly; she is very handsome," added he; "and, my life on't, her friends would pay a good round ransom for her."

Albert, curious to see the fair one, followed his adherent to the audience-room, where he was told by Jasper that the father was an ecclesiastic; and on having him brought forward, his surprise was great to behold Jocelyn, the abbot of St. Mark;

and if astonished to see him, what was his emotion at recognising in the lady his loved, long-lost Sabina!

They knew him not; and collecting his firmness, he received them with great politeness, besought them to hush their fears, and be assured they should quickly be restored to their friends.

Though they put little confidence in the promises of a robber, they thanked him, and endeavoured to appear as easy as they could.

The restraint was quickly seen through by him, and he had them conducted to a chamber where they could converse without a witness, and gave orders that every attention should be paid to their wishes. When Sabina thanked him for the boon, and begged a blessing on his head, the thought of other days came rushing on him, and for once the robber was unmanned.

After they had left him, he sat down to reflect on what was to be done. The band had already marvelled at his conduct. Even if he told them all, could he expect that they would suffer the captives to leave? He had broken many of their rules, and they began to be jealous of their rights. He thought of the beauty of Sabina, and shuddered at her danger. A violent noise in the hall of carousal struck upon his ear. Hastily repairing thither, he entered as two of the best men in the band were about to attack each other with drawn swords. Stepping between them, he desired to know the cause of their dispute.

It seems that these men had been principally useful in taking the abbot Jocelyn and his niece. The charms of the young lady had made an impression on both men. One demanded her as his by right, and the other that everything was common in the band.

Albert trembled for his beloved, at the same time sternly bidding them remember that he, as captain, had first choice.

"Granted," said one of the men; "and if you demand the abbot, why take him, and kill him as thou wilt; but, in all cases, a female prisoner is, according to the laws of the land, the property of the society; and if thine by first claim, must be ours in turn after."

"An excellent law," said Rufus, now lieutenant; "an excellent law, as the intent is to keep all females from amongst us, as likely to cause quarrels and ill blood. And who, but under particular circumstances, as this, where she could not be separated from the male prisoner, would bring a female here, knowing that, if the least contention rises, I have the power to restore order by burying my dagger in the fair one's heart. Such is the law, and I will here strictly do my duty. Therefore, captain, when the muster-roll is called, let the girl be brought forward, and I will do my duty to the band and to yourself, as well as saving the poor girl from worse than death."

The band applauded his resolution.

Albert stated that their ransom would be paid. The band, with one acclaim, cried out, that as it was a monk and a woman, they would not take ransom, as they were certain to betray them.

The abbot and Sabina were condemned to die in five hours by the general voice. Albert was compelled to acquiesce, and undertook to prepare her for her fate. The rangers now dispersed to their several duties, leaving their wretched captain overwhelmed with grief and terror.

What could he do against the collective force of the band? He could not see her die; and any attempt to save her on his part would only bring death on him, and fail of protracting her fate a single hour. For some time he sat in a kind of horrid stupefaction, then, rising hastily, proceeded to the chamber where they were confined.

On entering, he gazed on Sabina, and thought she looked more lovely than ever. The girl was ripening into the woman, like the modest bud bursting into the blushing rose. Apologising for his rudeness, he took Sabina by the hand, and intreating Jocelyn to be under no alarm for his niece's safety, he led her into the next apartment, which directly communicated, an oak partition only dividing the chambers. When they were alone,—

"Sabina," he cried, "have you no remembrance of me?—have my voice and person changed so much in a few years that you know me not?"

Sabina gazed on him with surprise and alarm—for his excited manner was calculated to inspire any female with alarm. She feared his intellects were unsettled. He struck his forehead with his clenched hand, and walked to and fro in agony, as she declared she knew him not.

"No, no," he cried. "I am forgotten—despised! and the loves of youth are ridiculed by maturity. Have you no remembrance of Albert Durand?"

On hearing the well-known name, Sabina started—seized his hand, and, with her eyes, ran rapidly over every feature; and then, as though by some turn of the countenance, suddenly convinced, she uttered a faint scream, and but for his extended arm, must have sunk to the earth.

The shriek brought the abbot into the apartment, who was much surprised at the scene before him, but more so when he heard Albert exclaim,—

"Yes, dear Sabina, Albert Durand!—falsely proclaimed as dead by the villain Arnold, and supposed to be buried in the monk's cemetery, at St. Mark's. The coffin was without an inhabitant. I am your once-loved Albert!"

Though Sabina plainly heard all that he had advanced, it was some time before she could get the better of the surprise, which may not be wondered at when Jocelyn informed Albert that he firmly believed that he had read the funeral service over him, and that for seven years he had been considered as numbered with the dead. Albert, in as few words as possible, told all that occurred to him at the castle, and his subsequent adventures, omitting mention of his guilt and crimes, with the exception of the death of Arnold, whom, they informed him, had been found by some of the baron's retainers, and being still alive, was carried to the castle, where he died, calling on Albert, and speaking so incoherently that all conceived he had some hand in the poor youth's death. Stephen had kept the secret, and Walter had been killed in hunting. The countryman that lent Albert the horse, and the two youths of Stonor, all swore to having seen Albert, and for a time, as their veracity could be depended on, they were believed, till years passed over, and he came not, nor was he heard of. The monks of St. Mark kept it a profound secret that he was buried in the cemetery.

Both Jocelyn and Sabina, though rejoiced to find Albert alive, were inexpressibly shocked to find him captain of banditti. Alas! they know not then their own dangers.

In as brief and delicate manner as he could, he told Sabina of her danger and her uncle's, and when she stood the picture of despair and terror, he knelt by her, and bound himself by the most solemn vow to preserve her from both death and violation; unawed by the presence of her uncle, he took her hand, and pressed it to his lips, bade her remember the night when she promised to be his for life.

"Ah! that night!" he cried; "that fatal night!"

Jocelyn now interrupted him, as his anxiety for his niece was overcoming every other feeling. As though electrified by a sudden thought, he pressed the hands of both, and begging them to be composed, and hope for the best, he made his way to where he had left Cyril Gaveston. He instructed the youth to engage the attention of the band, and while he did so, Albert, made his way to the store-chamber, and secured a strong decoction of poppies that had been prepared, by the leeches to soothe the agonies of the wretches beneath their care, for surgery was but in its infancy, and the instruments of these robber surgeons were but a rude saw, an axe, and a knife; taking this with him, he went to the hall of carousel, and into the well filled vessels of wine poured a certain quantity of the powerful decoction. He had often witnessed its effects on the wounded, and was surprised to see how small a quantity overcame the strongest man. Fearful lest the wine should taste of the noxious weed, he mixed the wine and brandy together, profiting by the distance the servitors had to fetch the food from,—the time they took in going to and fro. This was the duty of four men, who performed it alternately with four others, and it was while they were preparing the feast that Albert made his attempt.

At length the bell gave warning, and the band assembled at their accustomed board. In two hours from that Sabina was to die.

As though nothing had transpired, or was expected, Albert took his seat, and never did he urge the pledge, or teem the cup, as on that meal. He had cunningly a black jack before him, whose contents were undrugged. He set a worthy example, and during the rough gibe and wondrous tale, his followers imitated his example well; but one found fault with the taste, and that was the robber that had first claimed Sabina; but none objected to the strength.

Ere an hour and a half was over one half of the band were buried in sleep, and the rest were quickly dropping off.

Albert called Cyril to him now, and gave him his instructions, and the youth retired to obey them. Rufus, who was surprised at the unusual drowsiness of the gang, struck the table with his partizan, and with a loud voice bade them follow him to the hall of justice.

Half confused with the power of the opiate and the strength of the liquor, which alone prevented them from guessing the truth, their brains being in chaos, they rose from their seat, and, followed by as many as could stand, they staggered from one room to the other, till they reached the hall of justice. Albert followed, and as he saw the last man enter, he threw the massive door to, and knowing that it fastened on the outside, he shot the bolt, and fastened the chain across, making those within all prisoners. Quick as thought he now sought the chamber where Sabina and her uncle were confined. The robbers at the table yet slept; those engaged in the culinary duties were far distant. Swiftly he led Jocelyn through, and carried Sabina in his arms. Making his way over the prostrate bodies of the sleeping rangers, they quickly reached the stable, where Cyril had Jocelyn's horse prepared, which had a pillion behind for Sabina, it being the general mode of travel for ladies in those days; and when taken by the banditti Sabina and her uncle were on their way to London, accompanied by five retainers, that were slain by the gang. He also led one for himself, as Albert had in a few words told the abbot his story, and the worthy monk wishing to snatch the youth from the jaws of perdition, he was to accompany them to Richborough, and act as a guide through the forest.

Cyril had taken a pitcher of wine from the table, and drugged the contents, but the time being brief, when they arrived at the portal with their horses, they found the sentry there well prepared with wine, but not so overcome as not to be aware of treachery, which he was about giving notice of, when Albert sprang forward, and buried his dagger in his throat. The door was now opened, and the party issued out with the two horses. The voices of the robbers were heard; not a minute was to be lost; ere they could mount they would be upon them. Albert shut the door, and stood within, determining to defend the pass till he was certain they must have cleared the wood.

He was right; it was the robbers, who, discovering the trick played upon them, had contrived to force the door, and, roused by the event, were in pursuit like blood-hounds after their prey. On reaching the portal, and discovering Albert, their rage knew no bounds.

"Traitor!" they cried, "you have deceived us—you have betrayed us!"

"'Tis false," cried Albert. "Who dares to say I have betrayed you? I preserved the good and innocent from death and dishonour: though accused of my crimes,—a vile, degraded wretch,—yet for them will I devote myself, and suffer ye to hew me into pieces ere you pass to harm them."

"Down with him," cried fifty voices, infuriated at the trick that had been played upon them, and their worst passions set at work by the potent drink they had taken.

Albert, planting himself firmly with his back against the door, parried the blows of above twenty assailants, and in return made nine bite the dust, when a sound was heard, which had the effect of paralyzing all, and each stood transfixed in the same position. It was a loud flourish of trumpets, the sounds of horses' hoofs, and heavy tramps of armed men. In a minute after a violent blow came against the door, shaking the very wall.

"The troops—the soldiers—lost! lost!" was the cry.

Forgetting the past, Albert placed himself at the head of the rangers, and exhorted them to be firm, and boldly meet the danger. They strove to bar and barricade the door, but it was dashed to splinters by battering irons, and the king's troops rushed in. At first the robbers had the advantage, the passage being narrow, but the overwhelming number of the soldiers forced like a torrent all before it. At the large open space near the stable, the muster place of the band, the action was renewed, Albert cheering his men on; but, alas! the poisonous drug he had given them unnerved their intellects. They quickly fled, and sought shelter in the different apartments, where they were pursued by the soldiers, and throwing down their arms, they called for quarter. Albert, who had performed prodigies, resolved to sell his life dearly, and maintained a retreating fight. Hemmed in by numbers, at length stepping backwards, his foot tripped, and he fell; a dozen of his antagonists threw themselves on him directly. He was secured, and fast bound, and afterwards confined in the very chamber from which he had so lately released Sabina and her uncle.

The cave, and all its treasures, were now in the hands of the king's troops. Albert bethought him of the words of Rufus when he first was made a member. What had become of that worthy he knew not. He had seen him fall, and afterwards covered with gore, trying to defend the door of the great hall. After lying on the floor some time, he felt his wounds exceedingly painful, and a raging thirst. On the entrance of a soldier or petty officer, he called to him, for Heaven's love to give him some water, something to lie upon, and one of his own leeches to look to his wounds. As commander of the vanquished party, he considered himself entitled to so much by military courtesy.

"Wretch! dog!" cried the soldier, who afterwards turned out to be an officer, and the very same Sir Thomas Mostyn that he had enlisted with at Canterbury seven years ago. He had changed much in the time, and not for the better. His face was bronzed, and his forehead bruised and battered, and in fine, he was as much changed as Albert. "Thank Heaven that thou art fallen into the hands of the merciful, and not hacked into a thousand pieces on the spot—a fate too good for any one of your murderous gang."

"Does it become a soldier like Sir Thomas to insult the fallen? A rose has fallen from your chaplet, Sir Thomas," said Albert, raising himself on his elbow with extreme pain.

Sir Thomas stepped back a pace or two, and looked at the prostrate captain; then advanced, and gazed in his face.

"And who art thou," he cried, "that know Sir Thomas Mostyn—surely thou wert never soldier of mine?"

"No matter," feebly answered Albert. "I am your fellow-creature, and as a Christian knight, you are bound to show compassion."

Sir Thomas made no reply, but left the chamber. In a little while after some men entered, bearing a lamp, a rude mattress belonging to the men, and a large horsecloth, with some straw; these they put down with some show of tenderness. After making it up like a bed, they raised him and placed him gently on it. His limbs were stiff with gore. One of their own surgeons came and dressed his wounds and cleansed them. Water was plentifully allowed him, and a little wine and some provisions sent from the table of the officers who were now feasting in the place where he had so lately sat as a head and principal.

The next day he was commanded to give up the keys, and inform them where the treasures lay. In this he obeyed, for he was in too great pain and too weak to offer opposition. On the third day after, he was told to prepare himself for London.

Though much recovered, he was, as may be conjectured, but weak. He now saw that they were reserved for public execution. He was permitted a change of clothes the day previous. All of value that he possessed was a purse indifferently filled, a gold chain, and the glass dagger mentioned in a former part of the narrative, and which, being small, he had contrived to hide in the quilted lining of his vest, and it had escaped the notice of those who had searched him.

He was now taken and mounted on a horse behind a trooper, and buckled to him by a strong belt; his legs were also confined under the horse's belly, and his hands behind him. The band, about forty in number, were mounted behind other soldiers in a similar manner; the rest of them had fallen, or since died of their wounds. As he saw not Rufus, he guessed he was dead, and envied him his fate. They were not suffered to speak to each other, and, preceded by colours and trumpets, guarded by two troops with drawn swords on each side, followed by the cross-bow men, and the treasure, which was considerable, they set off, halting the first night at Dartford, and the next morning they set forward in the same order; all the towns and villagers turning out their population to see the famous Kentish banditti, reviling and throwing stones at them till repressed by the troopers.

In this manner they passed, and were greeted at Greenwich, Deptford, and Southwark, till they crossed the ferry. Changing their guard, they were lodged in the several prisons, being obliged to be brought into the city at night-fall, lest they should have been torn to pieces by the citizens—not one of whom but had lost some friend or property in the course of time by this terrible band.

Albert was lodged in a prison by himself. All ceremony of a trial was waved. The crimes of these men stood confessed; and with arms in their hands they had resisted the king's troops. A certain day was fixed for the execution; and now the affrighted soul of Albert shrunk within him. He had not feared to meet death in the melee, but its slow approach was terrible. The shades of all his victims stood in terrible array; the lives he had taken and the blood that had been shed in very wantonness, when on their predatory excursions, now rose in judgment against him. He thought of Sabina—alas! she could not aid him. He had saved her, and she was ignorant perchance of his fate; for he had ascertained that the military had never seen them, so that they must have taken an opposite course; perhaps concluding that the sound of troopers was proceeding from the banditti in pursuit.

As each day passed, and the time drew near, the mental agonies of Albert were almost beyond mortal bearing. He had never tasted food since he had been in the prison, a little wine, and a very small portion of bread, being all that he had to support nature with. But his heart sickened at the thought of food.

"Why feed a corse? Why give the means of life to one who so soon must die? —'tis mockery."

Such were his reflections. In the few days of his imprisonment he had changed so much that none of the band even could have recognized him. His hair, once of the raven's wing, was grizzled o'er with the hoar-frost, not of age, but sorrow; grief indeed lay heavy at his heart; grief to think on what he might have been, on what he was; it was ambition and his passions he had to blame—his own rash temper had undone him.

On the evening previous to the execution, as he paced his chamber in all the feverish tremor of despair, he was told a holy father, in pity to his soul, had come to shrive him ere he was summoned to another world. The words struck like death upon the heart of Albert; faintly acquiescing, he threw himself on his couch, and the monk entered; his face was partly concealed by his cowl, he was aged, and his appearance commanded respect. The sun had sunk, that sun which Albert was never to see set more, and the declining day gave but an imperfect light through the small iron-barred windows of the prison. The monk, in mild accents, besought him to unload his soul, and pray for Heaven's grace; with a willing heart Albert prepared to confess. It was no true feeling of religion; a week since, and he had spurned the good father from him; it was fear, it was terror—a drowning man catching at a straw. He did confess, and the blood of the holy father curdled to hear him. In one instance, he told of plundering a house while the inhabitants slept, and then, in very sport, setting it on fire, devoting the helpless owners to perish in the flames. His black catalogue exhausted, he was surprised to find by the speech of the monk that he was weeping. Rising and looking full on him, for he had now removed the cowl, he recognized Jocelyn, the abbot of St Mark. Death would have been preferable.

"Wretched man," cried Jocelyn, "in thy boyhood I loved thee well; in youth

I sought to do thee offices of good; and even when I saw thee the companion and chief of lawless men, I hailed thy wish to serve us as the token of a heart yet to be reclaimed. Alas! wretched man, how canst thou meet the hour of death?"

"I cannot, dare not die! Save me! oh, holy abbot, save me, for the love of thine own pure soul. Save me, save me from myself."

So saying Albert knelt and, hiding his face in the abbot's flowing robe, wept the bitter, scalding tears of a despairing soul.

"Pray not to a poor worm like me, but to the Great Power, whose image thou hast wantonly destroyed," said the monk, rising; and holding the crucifix in his left hand, he pointed to it with his right. "By the blood of Him who died for us, thou man of many crimes, I charge you to repent. Cast away the heart that has disgraced thy bosom, take to thyself a heart of grace, and repent; repent, I charge you, by your soul's hope, repent!"

"What time have I?" cried Albert, despairingly. "Will the penitence of hours wash away the guilt of years?"

"The penitence of a moment, pure and perfect, will obliterate from Heaven's register a catalogue of crimes. But hear me, man of terror," added Jocelyn; "since I heard of thy capture, in pity to thy soul, I have essayed my utmost means. You saved my life! more, you saved Sabina from dishonour; I will not be ungrateful. The gaoler here is devoted to the house of Fitzormond; in the dead of the night a disguise will be procured for thee, and a trusty emissary will guide you to a place of safety. This prison is old, and it might be a prisoner less affected by bodily weakness than thyself might effect escape, so shall it be believed; and may Heaven, who sees the motive, pardon the deceit."

No tongue can tell, no pen describe, the transition from despair to joy depicted in the countenance, words, and actions of the redeemed wretch. He laughed and wept in horrid joy.

Allaying his transports by a suitable admonition, Jocelyn then spake to the sinner of his future life. As Adrian de Morven his name was branded, and as Albert Durand still insecure. He must live to repent. Jocelyn offered to take him, after the necessary noviciate, as a brother of his order; reclaiming thus his soul from perdition. On this condition he answered for his freedom.

However reluctant Albert might be to leave the world, and however unfit for a monkish life, he bowed in acquiescence to the holy father, who was now preparing to depart, when Albert unadvisedly asked if any of his companions could be preserved from death. Severely the abbot answered,—

"Would'st thou again plunge into sin? would'st thou wish to save these, the instruments of thy destruction, again to tempt thy soul? You ask too much! no more."

Fearing to offend the monk, Albert in humble speech craved pardon for an involuntary feeling. Jocelyn said,—

"Let me hope the feeling was good; I am content to think so. At the midnight hour expect further. Benedicite, my son."

The portal closed, and Albert was once more left to his reflections. Hope revisited his heart; but he was still a prisoner. The hours, which before had fled swifter than the hunted roe, now halted on a beggar's crutch. At length the time grew ripe, and the door opening, a bundle was thrown into the room, and a voice cried "prepare;" opening it, he found a monk's gown, rope, beads, and rosary. He had scarcely concealed himself in it, ere a figure, standing in the portal, again cried "follow." Immediately pursuing its steps, they descended several flights of steps, and at length, by a different entrance to that which he had originally entered by, they emerged into the open air; they hurried on, keeping to the most unfrequented portion of the town. At length, turning a corner, they were suddenly met by a half military, half municipal body of men, in those days termed "Watch and Ward." The heart of Albert sunk. The principal, challenging Albert's companion, said,—

"Ho! what have you there?"

With admirable promptness of mind, the guide answered,—

" A friar going to pray to a dying man."

" Pass, father ; God speed you," was the reply.

" Benedicite," cried the mock father ; and the parties separated, each on their way.

They now made their way to the Chepe ; and, after turning down an obscure street, they stopped at a low-roofed house, with a far from prepossessing exte-

rior, and all the windows barred or otherwise secured with heavy shutters, covered with iron plates, and the door the same. While his guide knocked at it, Albert could not help thinking that the domicile he was going to strongly resembled the one he had left, except that it was not built so high. After a tedious pause, the sound of the removal of bars and chains was heard, which, from the noise, appeared to be numerous. At length the door moved on its hinges, and the figure of a decrepid Jew presented itself, holding a lamp ; at the sight of the unbeliever Albert started, he was brought up to hold the race of Israel in abhorrence, yet he continued silent.

"Aaron," cried the guide, "behold the party Jocelyn of St. Mark recommended to thy care."

"Any friend of the good Jocelyn is welcome to my poor house; but this, in especial; I pray you enter, good sir."

Albert turned to thank his guide, who had just placed a paper in his hand, but to his astonishment the figure had vanished. Perceiving that the Jew stood in courteous politeness waiting his entrance, he immediately went in, and the Jew shut the door, securing it with a variety of strong chains and bolts. He then led the way to a chamber, and pointed to a chair. Albert, considering that the holy habit was contaminated as well by his own wear, as the presence of his host, immediately took it off, and throwing it across its back, sat himself in the seat proffered by the Jew, still marvelling in his mind, how a connection could exist between a proud lord abbot, and a degraded and cursed Jew. Aaron now produced a basket, which he placed upon the table before Albert, saying,—

"I fear you would not like to eat with one of Israel's tribe, and this was brought by one of hine own people for thine especial use. I may not touch of food, or the vessels thereunto belonging on this day, therefore I pray you pardon me, if I play not the attentive host I would wish to be. There thou wilt find anything thou mayest want, placed by Rachel, my wife, for thy use."

With this, the Jew pointed to a cabinet close at hand, filled with goblets, platters, and all things wanted for a meal. The basket contained wine and edibles of the first quality, a most grateful surprise to Albert, who, as danger retreated, felt appetite return. Just then the paper his guide had given him occurred to his mind, he had thrust it into the bosom of his tunic; he drew it forth, and by the flame of the lamp, read these words :—

"Dear Albert—You are safe. My good uncle will give thee notice when to leave London. I have left that which will, I trust, repair your wasted form. I have seen you—I have spoken to you. I have seen you out of the house of bondage, into that of safety, and now, Albert, we meet no more. May Heaven bless thee. Sabina will keep her vow, but she can never be Albert's. Friend of my youthful heart, farewell !   "SABINA."

Albert groaned in agony. He had walked from his miserable gaol to the Jew's, with the idol of his affections, with Sabina herself. He started up with an intention of seeking her, till the impossibility of such a thing occurred to his mind. He cursed his own folly, and sat down in agony of heart. Not eating, the Jew courteously asked him if he had finished his meal. Albert could not eat. He passively removed the different articles, according to the Jew's prejudice, into the cabinet, after which, Aaron locked it, and gave him the key. Albert smiled in derision at the idea of a Jew's honesty. The basket which had contained the viands was on the table, being too bulky to be put into the cabinet; and, indeed, of two little value to be of note at all. The Jew, who had taken it up to remove it from his board, shook it, and calling the attention of Albert, told him it was not emptied. The other made some pettish remark, but Aaron in the same strain of suavity, begged him to examine it, at the same time putting it into his hand. To rid himself of the Jew's importunity, Albert emptied the basket on the table, when a well-filled purse dropped out before them. The eyes of the Jew sparkled, though it was not his, and Albert felt a pleasing grief at his heart, when he thought of Sabina's attention, who had placed it there that he might not lack means of enjoying his newly acquired freedom.

The Jew showed him to a neat chamber, and bidding him good night, and to take care of the lamp that then flickered in its last rays, left him. Undressing himself hastily, he lay down to taste that which for years he had been a stranger to—a calm repose, in safety, undisturbed by care or conscience. Let it be remembered, he was a Catholic, to whom confession relieves of a burthen.

CHAPTER III.

ALBERT was aroused the next morning by Aaron, who, after tapping at the door, entered with some garments over his arm.

"My good friend," he cried, " your excellent patron and myself have consulted, and he has honoured me so far as to approve of my humble suggestions. You are to put on these vestments ; they are humble, but good, and whole, and will conceal you better than your own, whose appearance cannot hide, but attract observation. You can reserve your own clothes, or I will buy them of you." Albert could scarce refrain from smiling. " Those are also your own. You will pass by the name of Ernest Travers, the son of a decayed Danish merchant, and my workman. I am a goldsmith by trade, and will induct you into a sufficient knowledge of it, that you may appear to be busy in the craft when any call ; otherwise you are master of your own time. My wife Rachel, who is a creature far younger than myself, whom I have taken as a handmaid, will show thee the same kindness as myself. Here you may sojourn for a month, at the end of which time you will proceed to the monastery of St. Mark. Attire thyself, and come down—we wait breakfast for thee, Ernest Travers."

So saying, the friendly Jew left the room. Albert could not but be grateful for the attention that had been paid to his welfare. When dressed, finding the necessary implements, he curtailed the appearance of his hair and whiskers, so that when his toilet was completed, he was as different as possible from his appearance of yesterday. His dress consisted of a coarse black cloth jerkin and trunks, with a round cap of the same cloth. His hose were grey, and his puffed shoon gave him a formal appearance, which his close cut hair and whiskers seemed to corroborate. On descending into the same room where he had sat the night previous, he found Aaron and his wife, as already stated, younger than himself, so much so, that she was by all strangers taken for his daughter. She was extremely pretty, and of a most winning address, and did the honours of the meal gracefully, and to her husband's credit, to whom she paid the same attention and deference that a child pays to its parent. The simple meal, which consisted chiefly of the produce of the garden, to which Albert added the remainder of his supper—hot water slops, as has before been mentioned, being a stranger in merry England of the olden time. They then, Aaron and Albert, repaired to the workshop, which was dark and smoky. Crucibles and tools belonging to the trade filled the shelves, and several curious antique busts and vessels of precious metal, stood about in different stages of repair or alteration. The branch of the business to which Aaron directed the attention of his new workman, was that of chasing, which in a plain way he soon got to understand ; also the sharpening of the tools, stones for which purpose, and emery, were in a portion of the shop, allotted for their use. To either of these occupations he was to apply himself when any strangers entered the premises, or to avoid the curiosity of his fellow-workman, a youth named Enoch Baldwin, a Christian, from a Jewish mother, who had married a Christian husband. This youth was curiosity personified, and so fond of chattering, that it required the utmost authority of Aaron to keep him silent at his work, or from running forth into the street when aught happened to challenge his attention. The new comer, as may be supposed, excited all his propensity. Albert could not refrain from smiling at the metamorphosis of the robber captain to the goldsmith's apprentice, though he soon had cause to confess its efficiency. He had not been a quarter of an hour in the shop, during which, Enoch had asked him about twenty questions, when a man came in for a silver jug, which Aaron had to restore to its pristine splendor. It was handed to him by the Jew.

"Well," said the man, " it looks smart. By my faith, you are a cunning craft, old Aaron, and when a killing of thy people happens in London (a great massacre of the Jews having a short time previous taken place at York, and they were suffering generally throughout the kingdom), you will be spared for thy good workmanship. As I live, the bilge that mistress made by throwing it at master's head, is not to be seen. Dear me, how bright it looks—the grapes seem just as if they were alive. Oh! you should have seen the thieves hung this morning—twenty on em, and there's twenty more to dance upon nothing next Friday; but hav'n't you heard about the escape?"

"Escape!" said Enoch. "No—what's that? Who's escaped, Goodman Durden?"

"Why," said the other, " the great cock captain of the whole gang. He was put in the Old Gate prison, and this morning, when they went to fetch him out, to stretch his neck a bit, the nest was empty, and the bird was flown."

Albert and the Jew stole a glance at each other. " Why, how could he get away?" asked the curious Enoch.

"Ay, there it is," was the rejoinder. " How could he get away? but, how-somdever, he did get away, 'tis said. He escaped at one of the windows, and sure enough the bars were wrenched out. Sampson Gurney, of the watch and ward, says that he can't have passed them, and the old gaoler swears that he had all the keys under his pillow; but gone he is, and the soldiers are after him everywhere, and are going to search the city, and as I live, here comes a set to search your place, Master Jew."

Albert turned pale, as four persons in military cloaks entered the shop.

"How now, Hebrew dog! hast thou taken a bribe to hide your friend?"

"My friend, gentlemen!" meekly said the Jew.

"Ay," says another, "I warrant me you Jews get rarely by such as him. You buy the plunder, and pop it into your crucibles. I marvel that the king don't issue a proclamation, for you all to be popped into the crucible yourselves. What persons have you in your house?"

"Myself and my wife Rachel," said Aaron, " and these two young men, my workman and apprentice, and this good gentleman, one of my customers," pointing to the first, Durden, who directly said,—

"Yes, sirs, I'm a good gentleman customer—I belong to Master Pounce, the scribe, and I come for his silver that his dame broke his head with, last Thursday was a week. I ain't a robber captain."

"No," says one, " you're only a thief in a small way."

This coarse sally provoked a laugh from the others, and sent the discomfited Durden out of the shop. Two now ascended the stairs to search the house, pretty Rachel conducting them. The other two remained in the shop.

"'Tis impossible the rascal can long escape," said one; " the pursuit is too hot, and the right boys are after him. So accurate a description is given of his person and his clothes, he must soon be taken."

One of them now looked full in the face of Enoch, and said,—

"You are not he, for you look like what you are."

"What's that, master soldier?" cried the other, endeavouring to look innocent.

"A fool," said the other, " and so you'll remain."

They both turned away with a loud ha! ha! leaving the offended apprentice ludicrously chap-fallen. One of the men fixing his eyes on Albert, cried,—

"Hilloa, Gabriel, what in the name of Lucifer do you call this?"

The blood paused in the veins of Albert.

"Who the devil are you?" said the other, bringing his face almost to touch Albert, who in a pretended stutter, said,—

"He was workman to master Jew."

"Where do you come from?"

"Glo-u-cest-e-er."

"Gloster, eh?" said the second. " Never was such a scarecrow as you seen in Gloster. What a head carved after the family bowl. And—eh? stop. Here's a cut just above the forehead, eh, Gabriel—the very—how the devil did you come by that?"

The Jew immediately took it up, and said,—

"That Ernest, when a boy, had been severely hurt by a fall, and a flint entering his forehead, caused the scar."

"Humph! it may be," said the soldier. " He don't look much like a captain. I should like to look at his left shoulder. I myself gave the rascal Adrian the cut six years ago and better, and when he was examined by the leech, it was I that found out he was the same rascal. Come, strip, sir, strip!"

The consternation of Albert and the friendly Jew was great, when at the moment a scream was heard, and Rachel, running down stairs, said,—

" That the gentlemen above had been rude to her."

The two immediately appearing, Aaron protecting his wife, bitterly inveighed against them for offering so gross an injury to a man in his own house. The only answer he got, was a cuff of the head from one, and a pull of the beard from the other, while Rachel was borne from his arms, and rudely embraced by the first, who passed her on to the next, and so following, the poor Jew being in an agony of emotion, which afforded food for the laughter and derision of his tormentors. Albert not being able to see this with calmness, struck the one who then held her, and was proceeding to greater liberties, a blow that sent him reeling into the street. A cry of horror escaped from the lips of Aaron and Rachel, while the soldiers immediately turned all together upon him.

"Who was he—a d—d Jew?" they asked.

"No," he said, calmly ; " but he was an Englishman, who would never stand by and see a woman insulted by men that were a disgrace to any country."

The soldiers now drew their swords, and the one that had been struck making a furious cut at him, Albert stepped back, and coolly parried it with an iron rod he happened to see near him, calling them to beware—that they had conducted themselves in an unjustifiable manner, and would be made suffer for it.

They all four now raised their swords to cut at him. Aaron, his wife, and even Enoch, stepped between ; but, doubtless. murder would have been the consequence, but for the appearance of an officer that entered at the moment. At a word the swords of the men were sheathed instantly. The officer angrily demanded the reason of the tumult. The moment he opened his mouth, Albert recognised Sir Thomas Mostyn again, and his last hope seemed to fail him. Retaining his presence of mind, he briefly stated the whole affair. Sir Thomas severely reprimanded them, as it appeared that they were also intoxicated. To prevent the soldiers taking upon themselves, in the search, to insult or rob the citizens, the officers were then going round.

" The search was sufficient," said Sir Thomas. " I have seen the robber Adrian more than once, and none here bear the slightest likeness to him ; so begone."

The fellow who had noticed the cut now came up to Sir Thomas to tell him, when that officer, offended that his orders were not instantly obeyed, he immediately pushed the offending subordinate out of the place, who was quickly followed by the rest, glad they had got out of the affair so well ; for by Sir Thomas's conduct, they knew that Aaron was what was termed a privileged Jew, or one that had lent money to the state, which was, in fact, the case.

Courteously apologising for the conduct of his men, Sir Thomas left them well pleased at the termination of the affair ; but it had better never have chanced, for it was the cause of ill to come.

From that day, Rachel looked with kindness on Albert, and Albert became insensibly pleased with the handsome Rachel. As he now seldom went into the shop, he would sit with her for hours, listening to the tale of Israel's tribes, and their history, scriptural and profane. Aaron, who would often join them, saw nothing in this but the curiosity of the youth, and desire of Rachel to induce one Norman descendant to think well of Judah's persecuted race ; but friendship begat confidence, and in an evil hour Rachel forgot her husband's goodness, and Albert not only Sabina, but honour, gratitude, and respect for himself. He had now remained three weeks at Aaron's, and had heard of the search of the military after him, and of finding a body with the very dress and marks dead at the portal of the old cavern, now filled up and the land levelled. It was fully identified as Adrian de Morven ; and the last of the three rangers being now destroyed, all pursuit ceased.

Jocelyn had sent for Albert's dress, and Albert had no doubt that a dead body had been in it, and all things arranged to strengthen the deception. The termination of the present week was the period allotted for the return of Albert to Stoner. Jocelyn had already written to him, telling him that his being alive was known in Stoner, but none had the most distant idea that Albert Durand and Captain Adrian were one and the same person—that many who had asserted that he was alive before, now believed that they had seen him frequently, or, at least, they had told it to others so often that they believed it themselves, amongst whom Pierce Gherkin had been the most positive. It was no wonder, then, that though startled at the first appearance of Albert, he received him so courteously. The mandate of Jocelyn gave Durand the utmost uneasiness; his bosom was torn by a tempest of conflicting emotions. He desired, yet feared to return to the vicinity of Richborough; the thought of the castle was Heaven, and the monastery filled him with grief and disgust. He seemed tied to Rachel, and yet thought only of Sabina; but he had no alternative. Rachel would have fain had him fly with her, but he had been a man proscribed too long. In Jocelyn's plan he saw peace and safety, and before his noviciate might expire, some chance occurring, would ——

Here his meditations were broken in upon by Rachel; she had just heard from Aaron the day fixed for Albert's return. Bathed in tears, she threw herself into his arms, and besought him not to leave her. Now, indeed, did Albert bitterly curse his own folly. He saw that he must grossly dissemble, as Rachel's grief and emotion must be perceived by Aaron, whose penetration would soon discover the cause. He well knew the revengeful nature of the Jew. A word from him, and Albert would die the death of a wretched malefactor.

He endeavoured, therefore, to tranquillize Rachel, telling her that she had heard but the abbot's mandate, that he was her's ever, and would not consent to Jocelyn's plan.

" Why then refuse to fly with me ?"

Albert attempted to point out his want of means to do so.

" That be my care," cried the wily Jewess, and unlocking a cabinet that stood near, produced a coronet of diamonds, each of great value, and a casket of precious stones, with two bags of gold. " These," she cried, " I know where to double, ay treble ; take them and me, and fly."

The sight changed Albert from himself—it was the robber captain gazed ; in a word, he consented to the plan of the amorous Rachel. To-morrow she was to procure as much gold from the Jew, either with his knowledge or without, as the time would allow, and on the morrow night they were to bid London farewell. They now parted—the heart of Albert proved its baseness. He weighed in his own mind the best plan to agree to Rachel's proposition, and seek another land, or to persuade her to place the treasure in his hands, and for him to fly unencumbered. She dared not acquaint her husband, and he might yet face the abbot. The guilty pair had thought no ear had heard them or their arrangements ; but one, who never let aught pass unobserved, saw all—heard all. It was the apprentice Enoch, who hated Albert on account of the favour he seemed to stand in with the Jew, and his exemption from all shop duty, a thing he could not understand, but was resolved to discover the cause of. Accordingly, when Aaron went forth, he always narrowly watched the workman Ernest, and soon discovered the intimacy that prevailed between Rachel and Albert. For a time he kept the secret to himself, debating in his own mind how he should best turn it to account ; but he now found, that " the affair cried haste," and he must be quick. On Aaron's return, then, he assumed a more than usual mysterious look, and seemed lost to the objects around.

" What, wool-gathering again, thou soul of the half-blood ! to work—to work, or I'll make thee."

Folding his arms, and leaning against the wall, Enoch carelessly kicked a stool from his feet, and, with a knowing shake of the head, cried,—

" No, master, I cannot work, my heart is too full to work ; this is a wicked, bad, good-for-nothing, trust-nobody sort of a world, I see."

On Aaron's demanding what had thus moved his spleen, Enoch, in a most mysterious manner, led the old man by the sleeve of his gaberdine into the little room at the further end, which served as a sort of counting-house; there he told the astonished Jew the whole tale. At first Aaron doubted, till recollection supplied many circumstances of a doubtful character that had occurred lately. The lad, too, could not forge the tale, as he gave a full description of the cabinet, and jewels, even to their very colour. Desiring him, therefore, to be silent, he now sought his chamber and wept, and prayed for the souls of the guilty pair. He then, that revenge might not prompt him to some desperate or rash deed, left the house, and took a walk in the city,—under present circumstances a ramble in the wilderness. He spoke to others of his tribe, but no word escaped of his injury; he returned to supper—he came home unexpectedly, for he made no noise in passing through the shop, where in general his voice was to be heard giving directions, instead of which he directly proceeded to the supper-room, where he found Rachel seated on her seducer's knee, his arm round her taper waist. They were at that moment planning the murder of the old man as the most certain mode of obtaining the money. On his entrance, then, they started up in great confusion, which he pretended to take no note of; but beginning to talk of the court news, and other matters of the day, he gave an opportunity to them of collecting themselves, and also prevented them from suspecting that he was acquainted with their perfidy. The supper was unusually profuse, the wines of the first quality, and never did Aaron seem more solicitous to please.

Albert's heart smote him for injuring the peace of such a man; as for Rachel, she had no such feeling. When once the heart of a woman is abased, no crime appears too monstrous. They distance men, and run a race with fiends for supremacy in vice. When the meal was concluded, Aaron said,—

"Rachel, my beloved wife, I have held thee as my heart of hearts; yea, in my heart's core thou hast been my star, and I am joyfully content in thy brightness. I would here, in the presence of our good friend, for whose near loss our hearts are grieved, pay to thee the compliment and honour our kings did unto the beauteous queens of old."

So saying, he filled her goblet and his of rich wine, and taking a sparkling jewel from his vest,—

"This stone," he cried, "is worth England's crown, and with this precious gem I pledge thee." Near him stood a silver cruet, with patent vinegar of foreign lands. He dropped the gem in, and in an instant it was dissolved. He then divided it into the two goblets, his own first receiving the share, and then touching hers with his, he said, "Rachel, here's to thy love," and quaffed it off.

She was, of course, compelled to follow the example, while Albert in secret contemned the useless extravagance that might have ransomed a score of souls from slavery.

The conversation turned on Stonor and his quitting. While talking, he observed Rachel turn deadly pale; but he attributed it to the ungrateful subject they dwelt upon, and did his best to change it; but the Jew was not to be put from his point, and still kept asking questions of Richborough and its vicinity. Sandwich was at that time in its infancy, a wretched fishing-place, with a few huts in it. While thus engaged, Rachel suddenly screamed, and Albert, on turning with horror, saw that her face was nearly black; starting up, he was going towards her to take her hand, and inquire the cause of her sudden illness, when he was stopped by Aaron, who, knitting his brow, cried,—

"None shall assist her—she is a disgrace to our tribe; she hath shamed our faith by committing wickedness with the enemies of her fathers. The gem was a poison artfully contrived to resemble the diamond it counterfeited, the cruet had a false lip. I poured none into my own glass. She has swallowed all up, and now, ere many minutes, you will perceive her death—death in the agonies that a false and perjured wife should suffer."

A groan burst from the wretched woman.

"Ay, groan," he cried, "bad, wanton, wicked creature. Your plans are known. You would have murdered me, I have devoted you!"

Albert exclaimed, "Villain! wretch!"

" Hold, sir, hold ! Look on that woman, and your own heart will tell you
which of us is the villain."

A noise was now heard below.

" They come for you, bad man ;" take that, " throwing down a purse well
filled, " take it, 'tis yours ; but, remember, you leave this house with the curses
of its inmates upon your head. A false friend—an unnatural guest. A horse
awaits you at the back gate. Jocelyn saved my life ; nay, more, he saved what
was dearer than life. For his sake I spare you. In another moment this room
will be filled by kinsmen that on the word will doom the dead. Go—go, lest I
madden, and stain the Jewish character with a Christian crime."

So saying, he pointed to a ring on the flooring ; he pulled it—it was a trap-
door. As he descended Albert cast a look at the dying Rachel, and his heart
smote him. The door of the apartment opened, and he could plainly see the Jews
entering as Aaron closed the trap. He quickly made his way to the garden-gate,
and found the horse, mounting on which, he turned towards Kent, and prepared
to bid adieu to London.

In the mean time the wretched Rachel died before all her kin, reviled and
cursed, and was buried that night, as a being not worthy the rights of sepulchre.

Aaron was declared to have acted rightly. It is needless to say that the pretended gem was a sudden and subtle poison made into a gum, and by some
process coloured, and made to sparkle, by curious manufacture. The next morning the Jew's shop opened as though nothing had transpired, and no further
inquiry was made.

Albert journeyed by easy stages ; for Jocelyn had enjoined him not to put on
the least semblance of haste or alarm, lest he might attract attention, which
would perchance lead to a discovery. His thoughts dwelt on the late dreadful
scene, and his heart was heavy—another crime was added to the calendar of
his iniquity. On the third day he knew he should arrive by night, as the
scenery began to be familiar to him. In the lining of his vest he still carried
the glass dagger, now of little consequence, but he had intended to have used it
to save him from the scaffold.

The afternoon was cloudy, and as he approached the scene of his childhood the
storm began to threaten. It has been clearly shown that he did not reach the
gates of Stonor till after the time of closing, and his subsequent reception by the
tailor, Pierce Gherkin.

CHAPTER IV.

In the morning Albert was awoke by the birds singing in the branches of vine
that grew around his chamber window, and the sun that darted its warm rays
into the apartment, as though anxious to know if a man so stained by crime could
sleep. Having rose, and attired himself, cursing the quaint and ill-cut fashion
of his garments, on descending, he found his host at work, and his breakfast,
consisting of eggs, fruit, brown bread, and a bowl of milk, which he spared not.
During the repast the little tailor, who seemed to be very desirous to talk, but
not knowing how to begin, at length broke silence with,—

" Well, Master Albert, (Durand started, it had been long since he had been
so called) who or what could put it into the foolish people's heads that you were
dead ? Why, bless me, you have been seen by many—that is many have seen
you somewhere, and don't know where. I don't know where I saw you last
myself."

Albert paid more attention to his breakfast than his host, and Pierce
proceeded,—

" But good Lord, what strange fashions they have in London ! You came
straight from there, did you not, Master Albert ? and the cut of that jerkin would
disgrace the form of Dunder, the butcher of the Grange ; and then the cloak,
who ever saw a gallant in such a cloak ? I pray, Master Albert, give me leave to

alter thy vestments, and for the love I bear thee I will put them in more gallant
fashion nor you a doit the less in pocket."

Albert thanked him coolly, but the subject being unpleasant, hastily dismissed
it. The vision of last night, for vision he still deemed it, dwelt upon his mind,
and a something urged him to quit Stonar on the instant; but eight years were
now fast completing since he had quitted it before, and he had ample cause to
wish he had remained in it or its vicinity, so, preparing himself to wait on Jocelyn at the convent, he offered Pierre a suitable remuneration for his kindness;
but it was not till Albert had insisted on his taking it, on pain of offence, that the

See p. 39.

kind repairer of doublets would accept of pay for that which Albert ought to
receive, he contended, at every one's hands after so long an absence. Durand left
him looking at the money, and blessing him for his bounty.

On walking forth he saw Richborough again, towering proudly over all, and
all seemed to wear the self-same look it did on that eventful morn he left
entering Stonar a crowd of recollections of early days came over his min

gave pain when they should have excited pleasure. Several seemed to know him,
and addressed themselves as though to speak to him, but he shrouded himself in
his cloak, and soon reached the gate of the monastery. On inquiring from a
lay brother of the abbot, the former left him for a time, and returning, desired
him to follow, which he did, through well remembered passages and rooms, till
they came to the abbot's closet. On being ushered in Albert was most kindly
received by the aged ecclesiastic, who was evidently ignorant of the affair at
Aaron's, by the manner he received him. One thing excited Albert's astonishment; Aaron had, almost at the last moment, given Albert a ring to give to the
Abbot Jocelyn, which he said had been left to repair, the circumstance had
nearly escaped him, till he saw the venerable father drawing it from his vest;
he immediately presented it to him—it was plain, and set with a simple stone of
a dark or black hue, sprinkled with red spots. The moment the abbot received
this his manner altered, and he sternly demanded of Albert the health of the Jew
and his household, and when the other, with changeful face, and faltering tongue,
declared that all was well,—

"That Jew," cried Jocelyn, "is a man might be an ornament to any creed.
I owe him much, for though it hath been in my power to repay the debt in
worldly wise, and also to befriend him, still I can never repay his kindness to a
stranger. It was in Spain we first met; I was young, and had embraced the
profession of arms; I was left wounded in the field of battle, and afterwards
stripped by the wretches that live by robbing the dead. Some good creatures
wandered round to give aid and comfort to those who lived—such was this Jew.
He performed indeed a Christian office; he had me taken to his house, where I
received every comfort, yet this Jew had just been compelled to fly from English
persecution. It was long ere I recovered, and yet his kindness was unabated,
and when my strength was sufficiently restored, he gave me horse, clothes, and
money, and bade me ' God speed,' with tears in his eyes. It was not till many
years after that, when I had become the abbot of this monastery, one of the
richest in England, that, going to attend the duties of Parliament in London, I
there saw a mob ill-using a son of Israel, and the soldiers cheering the people on,
like dogs to their prey. In that Jew I immediately beheld my former friend; I
immediately dismounted, and throwing my stole over him, I dared any man to
take him from the power of the Church. I removed him to a place of safety, I
found that his house had been seized, and his property confiscated. Having returned to England on the death of his wife, by my power and interest I recovered
a part of his property for him, and contrived an arrangement by which, though it
cost him money, he has been ever since protected from the harpies of state, and
seems as though he can never be too grateful, and yet 'tis I that am his debtor
still. I would, young man, you had given him cause to bless you; but, sir, the
ruby is not of the right blush."

Albert now saw plainly that the two in some way corresponded with each other
by means of the ruby, and he had brought his own sentence, or signal of disgrace. In fact, as he soon after was informed, there were two rings, one a
pale, the other a deep blush; by that signal it was that he knew Albert had forfeited the Jew's friendship.

Jocelyn now told Albert that he must commence his noviciate; ere he left him
Albert ventured to inquire for Sabina, and whether he could see her. In a tone
of voice that made the heart of Albert sink, and his blood run chill, the abbot
answered,—

"No, you have forfeited all hope of Sabina, even could the pride of our family
be forgotten. Sabina the wife of a mountain bandit! make your peace with
Heaven, and think of the world no more."

He was then allowed to return, and, after walking through the gardens for
some hours, he entered the refectory, and after donning the habit of the noviciate,
a white surplice, he was initiated in all the duties of his office. For a few weeks
he was treated with kindness. In the chapel of the monastery he in vain looked
round for Sabina—she came not. He was unworthy of her, and she despised

him. So would his brain work, till he was driven almost mad, and Jocelyn would make his duties lighter. He had never left the gates, and the abbot gave him permission to wander as he would. Assuming the habit of a lay brother, the time of his assuming the cowl being already fixed, the next day he saw Cyril, who informed him that the baron had been kind to him; but that he (Albert) was strictly forbidden to enter the castle on any pretext, until the day had passed when he should be admitted into the holy brotherhood. Sabina had been kindness itself to him; the name of Albert but seldom escaped her, and when he was mentioned she always wept, and retired to her chamber. Durand was in doubt whether the affair of Rachel was known to her, and on that account he feared to meet her; in Stonar and its vicinity she had many pensioners, and Albert could not refrain from haunting those places she was known to frequent.

Among the holy brotherhood were many who, like him, had been driven from society by their crimes. A number, too, were younger sons, or brothers, who had been put into the brotherhood, as young children are sent to school, to "keep them out of harm's way." Among such men, though practising the trade, and assuming the show of piety, there was but little true religion, and their private hours were spent in each other' cells in a manner little according with the strict rules of their order.

Abbot Jocelyn, as before stated, was a good and holy man, and discountenanced all sorts of debauchery in the monks, and from that was but little liked by them; but he was the immediate relative of the Castellan of Richborough, and also in high favour with the archbishop, and with the court of Rome, and report spoke loudly of a cardinal's hat promised. His power over the monks was great, therefore, and in Stonar he was looked upon as a saint on earth. Two of the brotherhood Albert was particularly attached to, one was an Italian, Father Antonio; and the other an Englishman, Father Urban. The latter was a man in his meridian, Father Antonio was farther advanced in life, and an invalid. Urban, and Albert, who, by the especial command of Jocelyn, was to take the name of "Adrian," when he should take the cowl, that he might ever keep the crimes in mind that he had committed under that name, were inseparable. Urban, as has been since remarked of a foreign royal family, in the lapse of years "had learned nothing, nor forgotten anything." He truly might be termed a wolf in sheep's clothing, yet in appearance he was sanctity itself, and his charity proverbial. He had endowed the monastery with a large sum and rich lands, as it was said by those who loved him not, solely with a view to keep them from his brother's children, who would have inherited them at his death. Such a companion could not but be hurtful to Albert—it was like putting fire to gunpowder. One evening, while walking on the beach, the same beach where Albert had seen the fearful figure, he thus recounted his adventures :—

History of the Monk Urban.

I am the son of a London citizen, and my real name John Beauchamp; my father was a merchant, who traded with Venice and Genoa. I was bred in comfort and, may be said, luxury; my younger days were marked by a predilection for mischief, and I cared little whom I made a victim of. Thrice, in the night, have I given the alarm of fire, and enjoyed the sight of the inmates making their way out of the windows in a state of nudity, and I always chose the coldest and wettest nights of the season; if any one broke their legs or arms, or was deranged for life, I enjoyed it as the greater joke.

I had one brother—whom I heartily hated, because he had taken the liberty of coming into the world before me—and a sister, who was reckoned the pride of London for her beauty. My mother was dead, and, by her last words, had recommended me to their loves. If anybody had any power over me it was my sister; and if I feared any one it was my father. I had not advanced far in my teens when I formed an acquaintance with Gilbert Brayle, a man of notorious character, that resided on the skirts of the royal forest of Greenwich. He had a sister, named Beatrice, worthy of such a brother; she was a beauty of the masculine order, and a liaison very soon took place. To supply her and her brother, I robbed home as much as I possibly could. My continual absence was noted, and I was questioned, but ever gave evasive answers, and found fresh pretences, all equally false.

My father had my elder brother christened after a rich relation. I was christened after my father, who, as it may be supposed, was more fond of me than my brother; and I artfully contrived whenever I committed a fault to fix it on Robert, which my father was too willing to believe, but that my sister, who would investigate the case, would often convince him against his will.

One May-day a royal hunt was proclaimed in the king's manor of Greenwich. My father, brother, sister, and all our household went out to see the king, and see the archers shoot. The night previous Gilbert and Beatrice laid a plan for me to rob my father's cabinet, and also the pantry of its store of plate. I at first hesitated, but they plied me with drink, and Beatrice was so lavish of her caresses, that I promised to do the deed.

Coming home, I struck across the royal manor, and saw a young female flying before an infuriated bull; the sight brought me to myself on the moment, and, drawing my couteau-de-chasse, I stepped in between them, just as the enraged animal was on the point of overtaking her. Calling out to her to stop and fear nothing, I struck the bull over the eyes; in the madness of pain it plunged furiously, tearing up the earth and grass, and endeavouring to make at me. I was not deficient of courage, and was always blest with coolness in the moment of danger; I kept at his side, turning as he turned, yet keeping his attention from reverting to her, and, watching my opportunity, buried my weapon just above his left shoulder, as I had seen the matadores in Spain— having often attended my father in his visits to that country and Portugal. The bull fell; and I then went to offer my services to the young female, who had sunk on a bank almost insensible.

Never had I seen so lovely a creature; her plain garments adding to her transcendant charms by the contrast. She thanked me in the sweetest voice I had ever heard; but, when she attempted to rise, I perceived she had sprained or dislocated her ankle, which had caused the bull to gain upon her. Perceiving the agony she suffered, I besought her to allow me to carry her home, or at all events to the nearest dwelling. She informed me that she was the daughter of Walter D'Arcy, one of the king's keepers, and that her parents resided a short distance from the spot.

She essayed to walk, clinging to my arm for support, but I immediately took her up in my arms, and scarce felt her weight, so proud was I of my burden. We soon, too soon for me, reached the keeper's house, where I was loaded with thanks by him and his wife, and also by the lovely Isabel herself. I felt that I could not, with propriety, stay longer then, but, requesting to be permitted to call the next day to inquire after her health, I left. As I made my way home, I could think of nothing but Isabel, and the contrast between her and the masculine Beatrice, whom I now wished I had never seen; I recollected, too, that Gilbert Brayle bore a deadly hatred to this keeper, and I reached home in no very enviable state of mind.

In the morning I was awoke by the merry horns announcing the royal cortege to be on its way. Our people were soon ready, and I was summoned to attend, but pleading indisposition they left me behind, one old female and a mere boy being only left to prepare for the dinner when the hunting party should return. And now my promise to Gilbert rose to my mind; as I, also, wanted money, and we were to share alike, I thought I'd take time by the forelock ere Gilbert arrived, who was to remain without, to receive the plunder. Making my way to my father's chamber, I found the cabinet that contained the gold, but knew not how to open it. I remembered, when a child, hearing that it was fastened· by a spring, but where, or how to be touched, I remembered not. After many unavailing attempts, I got an iron screw driver and an axe, and, with a deal of trouble, succeeded in bursting it open. The bags of gold (ten or twelve in number), soon presented themselves to my gloating eyes. I had already pocketed them in anticipation, and was proceeding to seize them in reality, when I felt a hand laid gently on my arm ; turning quickly round, I beheld my sister Madeline, and I blushed at the situation in which I was caught.

"John," she cried, "what are you doing?"

Fixing her full, dark eyes upon me,—so guilty did I feel myself that I could not even devise a lie.

"Dear brother," she said, "this is not your own action, but that of some wicked persons who are seeking to delude your youth, and ruin your good name. Would you rob our father—and so good a father?"

Base as I was, I felt compunction, and hung my head.

"Come," she cried ; "none know of this but me. If indeed you want money for yourself, I have a little, and it shall be yours, but let me not see my brother ruin his father and destroy himself : this shall be concealed."

"But how?" I said, doggedly. "It must be found out ; the breaking of the lock will speak for itself."

"Leave that to me," she cried ; "I will see that all is repaired unknown to our dear father ; only promise me, John, that now, having seen the enormity of your offence, you will for ever abandon the society of such persons, who would rob you of peace in this world and of hope in the next."

Bursting into tears, I threw myself on the neck of Madeline, and made a solemn promise, which I never meant to keep. Taking me to her room, she presented me with a purse, containing not a large, but far from contemptible sum, and, with many promises and protestations, I left her. I certainly had my eyes opened by this, and in secret resolved if possible to cut the connection with Gilbert and his sister ; but the principal inducement was not my sister's preaching, but my having taken a dislike to them,—they had outgrown my liking. I now made my way to the keeper D'Arcy's, to inquire after Isabel, whom I found much recovered, though still unable to go forth. Her father was abroad, attending on his majesty. The more I saw of Isabel the more I was enamoured. I remained talking to her and her mother, as long as the etiquette of good breeding would allow, and then left reluctantly. On my way through the wood, my thoughts engrossed by the form of Isabel, I felt a rough slap upon the shoulder. Turning, I saw Gilbert Brayle by my side, who said,—

"Hillo, young master, you begin soon to double in the hunt. You play me false, sir ; I have waited for you. You are either a coward, or a hypocrite, which shall I call you?"

Stammering, I made up a tale of my sister having been in my father's chamber, and her presence preventing me from putting my project in practice. Folding his arms, and knitting his brows, he sarcastically asked me if my sister made me seek Walter D'Arcy's cottage, and spend my time with the pretty Isabel. My changing colour sufficiently evinced my guilt, if so it might be called. However, collecting all my effrontery to my aid, I haughtily demanded what right he had to interfere with my actions, or dare to comment on my conduct.

"Dare ! quotha," he cried ; "dare ! my name is Gilbert Brayle, and most folks know that I dare do anything ; but to answer you categorically ; I have a sister, and if I have reason to suppose you mean to play her any rogue's trick, and having served your turn, turn her off, I wear a dagger ; you see it in its scabbard—its next sheath may be your heart."

I trembled for well I knew the villain to be determined, and to stick at nothing to compass his revenge. I therefore endeavoured to pacify, and, coward as I was, to buy his friendship, and gave him the purse that a sister's kindness had just lavished on a worthless brother. The sight of the coin, more than all the words, seemed to pacify Gilbert. He affected to believe all I said. When I told him how dearly I loved his sister, and that nothing should ever part us, he shook me by the hand, called me his dear brother-in-law, advised me to beware of the keeper and his family, who, he affirmed, were a bad set ; and then, with a significant grin, hoped I should be on the look out, for he should want some money soon, was sorry that he should be so troublesome, but that women were changeable, and that he knew I should not begrudge anything that was for the support of my dear Beatrice, and then, with a sort of half laugh, left me.

When I got home I repaired to my closet, and for a time gave myself up to the most bitter feelings and reproaches for my folly in first making myself the tool of such persons. All my liking for Beatrice expired, and a rooted antipathy supplied its place. When summoned to dinner, I felt as if I dared not meet the gaze of my family, but I dared not depart from the established custom, and endeavouring to throw as much composure into my appearance as I could, I descended to the dining-room, the paleness of my countenance serving to corroborate the account of indisposition I had feigned in the morning. I was received with kindness and sympathy, and introduced to Sir Edward Bonnington, an officer in the king's army, and captain, or head of the royal archers, a portion of which, with Sir Edward, were about to join the prince to punish an inroad of the Welsh, and to destroy the castles of the border chieftains. During the repast, my father commented on my being a younger brother, and that as I must carve my fortune with my sword, an opportunity now presented itself, as Sir Edward had offered to give me a command in his own company.

At any other time this would have been welcome news to me, but at present I could not help thinking it rather *mal-apropos*. However, I made a grace of necessity, and pretended great joy and gratitude for the offer, not without first making a most fraternal offer of it to my elder brother; but my father declined it, saying that Robert would have a good estate of his own, and had no necessity of embracing arms, as a profession, a speech that did not in the least augment my idea of brotherly love. I was to go into training on the morrow, as the forces were to rendezvous at Shrewsbury on that day fortnight. On my leaving the hall, my sister congratulated me on the appointment, at the same time observing, that the purse she had given me would assist in my equipment. When left to myself, though it cut me to the heart to leave Isabel thus, just in the infancy of our acquaintance, I saw, or conceived, that it would rid me, at least for some time, from the importunities of Gilbert and Beatrice, and the thought of that operated in reconciling me to the business. I failed not at the first opportunity to see Isabel, and luckily finding her quite alone, told her of my military expedition, and observing her concern for which, I threw myself on my knees, making a formal declaration of love for her, offering her my hand and heart, and asserting that I was the elder brother, and that I must possess a good estate. Walter, her father, at that moment coming in, we were taken by surprise. I, however, repeated the same to him, and was pleased to find that he did not quite object to my suit, the estate having its charms, as he told me he was resolved not to give his daughter's hand but to one who could well support her. Isabel, too, agreed to receive me as a suitor.

Having thus far succeeded, I left them, not without having some sore touches of conscience about the estate, though I was pretty certain they would not be able to ascertain the real truth, as my brother was a young man of retired habits, and I was seen chiefly about with my father. I could not summon hypocrisy sufficient to take my leave of Beatrice, and as I heard nothing of Brayle or her, I thought I had a good chance of leaving London without their suspecting what course I had taken. I was seated at supper with the family, when I was informed a female demanded to see me. I started from my seat, and my father sternly interrogated me as to the intruder. Making him some evasive answer, I left the hall, and soon discovered, as I suspected, Beatrice, who began in a vituperative strain, till stopped by me with a threat, that if she ever presented herself at the gate of that mansion, she never should see me again. She asked me how I came to see Isabel, and not to say farewell to her.

" But let her look to it," she added ; " the Brayles have a long account of vengeance to settle with the D'Arcy family, and this turn shall not be forgotten at the settlement."

I then endeavoured to pacify her, and told her I was going to Harwich for a month, and wished her to meet me there, carefully concealing from her that I was appointed to the army. She complained of distress, and not having seen Gilbert for two days. I had that evening received a sum for the purpose of completing my outfit. A part of this I was obliged to give to her, promising to meet her the evening following. Hastily taking leave of her, making the fear of interruption an excuse for my apparent lack of fondness, I at length got rid of her, and on my return to the supper-table, was greeted with looks of mistrust and curiosity.

"I understand," said my father, "that you are taken with D'Arcy the keeper's pretty daughter. I request that my house may not be made a rendezvous for unprincipled characters."

In a moment I saw the mistake, yet knew not how to correct it. I, however, warmly espoused the cause of Isabel, who, I asserted, was incapable of such conduct. In this I was supported by my brother, and so warmly, that I felt uneasy. I recounted the accidental manner in which I became acquainted with the D'Arcy family, which seemed to give general satisfaction, and the subject soon changed to that of my departure in the morning. My brother and sister had loaded me with presents, and my father had supplied me, if not liberally, at least sufficiently. He also provided me with a horse to bear me to Shrewsbury, where I might sell it, as, belonging to a foot company, I should then have no further use for it. In the morning, at an early hour, I set forth, after taking a tender leave of my family, my brother riding with me part of the way. About four miles from London, crossing a common, we were met by an old peasant woman, bending under the weight of a load of dried sticks, collected from the hedges. As she was directly in the centre, I called to her to get out of the horse-way. She looked up, and after fixing her gaze first on one, and then the other, to Robert cried—" To be pitied, yet blessed;" and to me—" To be envied, yet cursed."

The words, but more particularly the manner of the speaker startled us. As Robert had before stated his intention of leaving me here, I turned from the sibyl to take leave of him. After which,—

" Mother," he cried, " how far go you on this track?"

She answered,—

" Nearly a mile—to a poor, decrepid, aged creature, a pilgrimage;" to which the burden of the sticks added a sensible increase of toil and pain.

Dismounting, he took them from her aged head, and laid it across the saddle, by which she was able to support herself by her crutch. I sneered and mocked at my brother becoming the champion of the old beggar woman, whom I styled " Mother Shipton." He replied but by a faint smile. While shaking her palsied head, the old crone cried,—

" Well were it for thee, John Beauchamp, didst thou never become the champion of a younger woman. Soldier for Cambria, the curse of the bard be on you."

We then parted. I, on my route, and my brother in company with his aged incognita, for she refused to state her designation, at the rate of three hours per mile. I met Sir Edward at the first town, and, in company with a confused chaos and crowd of men of all arms, I made my way to Shrewsbury. No order was kept in the march, and it might be said that we swarmed along the road. On our arrival among the proud Salopians, the case was different ; we halted several days to give rest to the troops, and a passage of arms was appointed to be held for three days. As such a thing had not occurred in this part of the country, it drew great numbers to witness the joust. The prince, the Earl of Oxford, and Sir Edward Bonnington engaged all comers. For two days they came off victorious. On the third morning a knight in white armour, with the device of the sun bursting through a cloud, the motto, " Not to be subdued," rode into the lists. The knights and military men around whispered that it was a Cambrian knight, and an enemy, and therefore not privileged to break lance at a tourney ; especially where the heir apparent to the throne opposed his person, in contention. Hildebrand de Broose rose his battle-axe to strike him from the saddle, but was prevented by the prince, who contended as it was a passage of arms, free to all comers, no knight, and certainly no Christian knight, could be forbidden. During this time the white knigh sat on his courser giving directions to his esquire, and paying no attention to what was passing round him.

On the herald sounding the order of the day, he rode up to the knight champions' banners, and touching the last of the three shields of the defenders of the pass with the end of his jousting spear, he caracoled his milk-white charger till he wheeled him into his place. The shield belonged to Sir Edward Bonnington, who rode immediately to the charge. He was soon unhorsed, and the second shield being also touched by the white knight, the Earl of Oxford engaged with him, and several of the spectators accused him of taking unfair advantage. He rode with a battle-spear, while the other had the light tilting lance used in common by all knights, when not fighting *a l'outrance*. They both bled copiously, and the judge or marshal of the lists was on the point of throwing down his warder, when the earl was fairly lifted from his saddle by the spear of the white knight, and he was brought to the earth with a heavy fall. A piece of treachery was then discovered—the earl had a suit of complete armour under his coat of mail.

The stranger knight now challenged the royal shield, but the lords and gentry crowded round him, contending that he was not justified in risking his person, the kingdom's hope, against a man unknown, by appearance an enemy, and, probably infuriated by the late discovery, would retaliate on the next antagonist. In short, so vehement and positive were they, that the royal shield was withdrawn, and the marshal declared the tourney terminated, and the white knight the conqueror of the day; in compliment to the prince, none taking up the gauntlet (which, as customary on such occasions, was thrown by the challenger on the ground in the centre of the lists), though many burned to do so, ashamed of a foreign knight bearing away the palm at a royal tilt.

The knight, on leaving the lists, bowed to the prince, now in the marshal's seat, saying,—

"When next we meet again, your highness may have a better stomach for the fight;" and immediately rode off with his squire and banner-bearer.

The prince, enraged, gave instant orders for him to be stopped, and I, being the nearest in command to the party, rode off at full speed, followed by some half dozen more. But we were soon distanced, it not suiting the Welshman's interest to be brought back. His speech cost him dear some time after—the prince, afterwards the famous Cœur de Lion, wiping off the tourney disgrace in his blood.

It may be asked why Richard, so proverbially brave as he was, suffered himself thus to be insulted and persuaded by those around him not to resent the insult; but the case is easily explained. It had been whispered to the prince that it was his brother John, with whom he had for some time been at variance; and on that account, and that only, he suffered himself to be led to his seat.

I found Shrewsbury much to my liking. The army lay in camp—the royal party and principal officers taking up their quarters in the town.

Sitting in my tent one evening, the sentry announced two strangers, who entered in large horsecloaks and slouched hats, and on the men leaving us, they discovered themselves to be Gilbert and Beatrice Brayle.

So unwelcome was their appearance that I could not even put on a show of complaisance, but pettishly asked what brought them hither.

"Love induced me to come," said Beatrice.

"And revenge me," cried Gilbert, furiously stamping, no doubt to intimidate me; but I felt that here I was paramount; that their loud talking could neither be heard by father or sister, and any show of violence could be met by calling for a file of men, and denouncing them as traitors, which would quickly terminate their existence on the next tree. I therefore sternly asked Gilbert to whom he spoke, and what vengeance he alluded to. I could see he was somewhat dashed at my firmness, and commenced a long tirade against young men taking advantage of a brother's poverty, and a sister's beauty, and then, seeing one they liked better, casting off their first favourite, and betraying the brother to his mortal enemy.

I could easily perceive that the drift of this pointed at the D'Arcys; but not understanding what he meant by betraying, I asked an explanation, when Beatrice, with tears in her eyes, which she could command at any time, told me that I need not plead ignorance, since I, in order to obtain Isabel, and get rid of them, had betrayed Gilbert to D'Arcy, his inveterate enemy. The forest laws, since the conquest, were very strict, any offence being pardonable by the payment of fines; but killing a deer in any of the royal forests was punished by the loss of an eye, and often by death, in cases of an aggravated nature. Gilbert was known to be a deer stealer, and an arrow found sticking in the haunch of a stag, bore his mark, and the keepers were after him, and they seized his cottage, from which he had been compelled to fly, and which, though his own fault, he wished to ascribe to me, for

See page 49.

the sake of exacting money. I sympathised with them, but repelled the charge. Thus circumstanced, I was obliged to give them money, advising Gilbert to enter the army, which he partly agreed to.

Beatrice besought me to let her remain with me, until I proposed to put her into some convent as a boarder, till the times were more settled. She then agreed to repair to a relative's dwelling at Eltham, on the promise that I would come to her when the army returned.

Having thus, as I thought, again got rid of them, I let my thoughts wander to Isabel, and my future plans. We were now marched to Wrexham, and an engagement took place, where the Welsh were completely routed. The army established itself in head quarters ; and strong detachments, headed by men of ability, were sent to reduce the castles of the border chieftains.

Sir Edward, with a powerful force of horse and foot, set down before the castle of Rhap-ap-Howell, one of the most turbulent of the Welsh barons. So well were the belligerent leaders matched that little advantage was obtained on either side. The castle had a powerful garrison, and was well supplied. At length it came to a complete stand in tactics, each watching any unguarded movement that might give advantage, like two skilful chess-players, that had brought each other to a point. Irresolute they paused, afraid to move their men, till, as if by mutual consent, they relaxed, hostilities, each exhibiting seeming apathy, to lull his antagonist into security While this prevailed, I amused myself by wandering about the neighbourhood to see the different ruins and relics of antiquity. One day, having been to see a curious cross or pillar, on my return I was overtaken in so sudden a storm, and which threatened to be so severe that I was obliged to look round for some place of shelter. There was little fear of being surprised by the enemy, as the garrison, which consisted of the surrounding population, were close blockaded in the castle ; and the Welsh, since their last defeat, had no regular army in the field. I saw a building, which had in former times been of respectable note, but was now little better than a ruin, patched and propped up, seemingly as a domicile, by some very poor serfs. On approaching the portal, I heard the tones of a harp, and a tremulous voice singing the national air of

"The foe is on the Cambrian's land ;
Raise the battle cry :
The foe is on the Cambrian's land ;
Raise the banner high."

Confirmed by this that the inhabitants were no friends to the English, I debated within myself what should be done. The pelting shower soon put my doubts to flight, and I entered boldly. In the middle of the room sat an old man, blind with age, whose white locks were confined by the green ribbon that was bound over his eyes—a custom still preserved where, by lightning or fearful accident, the sight has been lost. A harp was at his knee, and a young girl of eight or nine years of age, apparently his grand-daughter, was spreading a board with a Welshman's simple meal. Both paused at my entrance, and the child, with affright in her looks, crept closer to the old man. In English, but interspersed with all the Welsh words I knew the meaning of, I told them my case, and asked for shelter. The request was granted by the old man, and the grand-daughter brought a seat for me. I could perceive that my presence was anything but welcome ; nevertheless, I was invited, courteously, to partake of the meal. No allusion was made to the position of affairs by either party. I confined my speech to inquiries as to relics of gonebye days I had lately been viewing. I found the old man intelligent, and, like all the bards of his day, a chronicle of the past. The repast being finished, and the storm still continuing, I felt excessively weary, and my host having offered me a pallet for the night, I accepted his offer, intending to make my way when day dawned to the camp.

I was shown by the little girl to a chamber, apparently directly over that in which I had been sitting. I was surprised to find the building so large ; but it was in a fearful state of dilapidation, and in treading over the crazy, worm-eaten floors, expected every minute to break through. A comfortable pallet and covering waited my use, and leaving the lamp, then nearly expiring on the floor, the child left me. Throwing myself on the couch, I busied myself in a train of reflections, till attracted by the harp of my host, to which he was singing some legend of the past. To sleep thus in the house of an enemy was incurring a risk ; but I knew the hospitality of the Welsh, and after eating with them, they are never known to betray a person, though he should prove the slayer of their own friend or kin—in this resembling the Moors, and other nations noted for good faith.

The vibration of the harp, and the exercise I had taken, soon lulled me into a deep slumber. How long I had slept I knew not, when I was awakened by the sound of voices, loud and angry. I was wholly in the dark. Starting up, I felt for the moment alarmed, but finding that my sword and dagger were safe by my side, I collected myself, and listened.

Observing the light gleaming through the chinks of the floor, I lay down and applied my ear to the largest, when, to my surprise, an Englishman's voice attracted my attention. Clearing the dust from the aperture, I was able to take a view of the kitchen and its contents, which filled me with astonishment and anxiety. The old man and his grand-daughter sat in one corner, in evident alarm. At the table, on which were spread the remains of a supper, sat Beatrice Brayle and two men, one of whom I recognised to be her brother, and evidently intoxicated. He held a drawn dagger in his hand, with which he was threatening the old man. Near the fire sat another person, wrapped in a horseman's cloak, but evidently a female. Her face was resting on her hands, and plainly evinced the state of her mind.

Gilbert was threatening the old man with death if he did not give up his gold and valuables, which the bard assured him was impossible, as he was poor as poverty could make him, the harp and humble moveables around constituting all his wealth. They seemingly had come furnished with their own liquor, as a large black jack stood upon the table, which Gilbert paid his devotions to, ever and anon filling a drinking horn : he proffered it to the old man ; on his refusing it, Gilbert said,—

" Come, no sulks, drink ; I tell you it will do your eyes good, and make you see."

" I see too much already," mildly observed the bard ; " I wish to see no more."

" Why, then, d—n ye, you shall feel," said the savage, at the same dashing it, horn and all, in the old man's face.

The child screamed, and clasped her arms round her grandfather to protect him ; the blood sprang copiously from a wound made by the violent concussion. While this was going on, Beatrice and the man at the table were whispering fondly together, he with his arm round her neck. The sight of this, and the wanton attack upon the old man, roused my vengeance ; but a third circumstance decided me—the cruel attack on the bard had caused the female to start from her seat to save him from further ill usage, and disclosed to my astonished eyes the features of Isabel D'Arcy. In an instant I sprang up, grasping the hilt of my sword. The violence of the action caused the flooring to give way, and my feet went partially through. I heard the bustle and exclamations of the party below.

" What the devil is that ?" said one.

" The devil come to set his foot upon us," answered the other.

Though forgetting where the door was, I made a plunge to that side of the apartment where I conjectured it stood, and fortunately hit upon it ; forcing it open, I hurried down stairs, but missing my footing, fell, and a sort of trap-door giving way with my weight, I fell a considerable depth, the trap-door breaking my fall in some measure, or I must have broken my neck ; as it was, I lay on a stone flooring, insensible from the effects of the fall. When I came to myself I could scarcely rise, from the bruises and contusions I had received. I was on the point of calling out, when I felt a hand laid on mine, and a low voice addressed me, which I recognised to be that of my aged host.

" Silence !" he cried ; " your life you have escaped by miracle. I have been feeling on the ground for your form, expecting you were killed. You have fallen through a trap-door, devised in former times for some purpose now unknown, so contrived as to open like a pair of shutters, and return again to its former position ; a wooden bar, or bolt, at the bottom, fastened it from yielding, except when reopened. That being worm-eaten in time, your sudden weight caused to yield ; the violent crash your armour made alarmed my unwelcome guests, and they searched the house. The trap matching so accurately with the boards around and which I took care they should not approach to tread on, baffled their search; their superstitious fears made them believe it was some supernatural noise, and had the effect to reform their behaviour in some degree. The storm still raging, they have been compelled to remain, and are now sleeping in the apartment you sat in, having secured the door.

"And their prisoner?"

"Alas! poor soul," added the bard, "she sleeps not. She has been torn from her home, and is, I fear, in bad hands. Will you try to escape? the storm has abated, and from the window of the room you slept in you may try to make your egress; from the door it is impossible."

"The villain shall die!" I exclaimed; but on attempting to draw my sword I found my arm was so badly hurt, and that the shoulder was so dislocated, that I could not raise it.

"Step softly, and follow me," he cried, taking hold of my left hand.

"But without a light," I cried, "how can you find ——"

"You forget," "he cried, "that light or dark is the same to me."

With that he led the way slowly, for I could scarcely move. We ascended a spiral flight of steps, and passing through a door, came into the passage leading to the kitchen, from which a faint light emanated, caused by the blaze of the turf fire. Stepping gently, we entered. Beatrice and the men were asleep, the former with her head on the table, and the two men extended on the ground. At sight of them I seized my mercy dagger with my left hand, with the intention of plunging it into the body of the nearest; the action, silent as it was, had not escaped the quick ear of my host, and he stretched forth his hands to prevent me.

"Are you mad?" in the same low key he cried; "if even your hand be steady sufficient, the noise will awaken the other, and your destruction will be certain."

Isabel, whom the slight noise of entering had disturbed from a half slumber, started up. My action instantly enjoined silence; but her emotion was so great at recognising me, that but for catching hold of the chair she had sat in, she must have fallen; the child lay on the foot of the harp, in the happy tranquillity of youthful slumber.

Gilbert had laid himself so near to the door, that could we remove the fastening, it was impossible to open it without his being disturbed. On the table was a lamp, which the bard, in a whisper, told me to light. Having done so, he led us out of the kitchen, Isabel leaning on my left arm. When in the passage, a sudden idea struck our host; and, leading the way, he sought a door at the back, at which he whispered Isabel to remove the bar; with our joint help—and mine was but feeble—we succeeded in noiselessly removing it, and emerged into the open air, but it was into a small court surrounded by walls. I gave up all hope, when the old man produced a rude, heavy ladder, which fell short of the summit; but, ascending, I stood upon the wall, while Isabel sat at the top, till, with infinite difficulty, with my weak left arm, but aided by the old man, lifting it as well as he could, we succeeded in getting it on the wall too. Balancing across it, hope warmed my heart, and escape now seemed probable; when, owing to my awkwardness, situated as I was I let it fall over; thus preventing all chance of getting either way. Fortunately the late rain had so saturated the ground that it made but little noise.

What was now to be done? In despair I gave all up for lost. The fertile mind of our host yet supplied an expedient, which proves that those who are deprived of sight, not having their attention distracted by outward objects, have cooler judgment and a quicker invention than those who see. He left us, and in a few seconds returned with a strong rope, one end of which he secured to the trunk of a perished tree, and succeeded in flinging it up so high that I caught it, and, with extreme difficulty, with one hand, let myself down. Isabel, to whom danger imparted a strength and courage foreign to her sex, held by the rope, and putting her feet against the wall, came down as well as a sailor boy would have descended his ship's side.

We had no time or means to thank the good old man scarcely; but ere we got over, he told us to keep to the left hand road, and sometimes think of Cadwallader, the Welch bard. Hastening, therefore, in the direction he told us, we beguiled the time by recounting our several adventures.

It seems, that one evening, going forth to meet her father at his usual hour of return, as had been her custom from childhood's day, she was suddenly seized by two men, who threw a cloak over her, and, hurrying her to some short distance, and placing a handkerchief in her mouth to prevent her from screaming, they forced her upon a horse, and fastened her to one of the men. In this way she rode all night, and in the morning alighted at a cottage, where she saw the woman Beatrice, who treated her with great unkindness, and but for the men she thinks would have destroyed her. Since then they had been travelling to that part of the country, though whereabouts she was she knew not. She understood, from what at times dropped from them, that they were taking her to some convent on the Welsh coast. She was in an agony to think of what her dear parents must be suffering on her account, and repeatedly asked me how long it would take her to retrace her steps to London.

While we were thus in conversation, we came suddenly to where four roads met; and though the moon was shining out bright, we could not tell which way to take—I had no remembrance of the spot. While thus pausing, uncertain which track to take, we heard voices directly in the direction we had come; in another moment the gallop of horses was plain to be distinguished. We were pursued. Striking to the left, we hurried on as swiftly as we could. We soon found that they had taken the same direction, and even could distinguish their voices.

Increasing our pace, we came suddenly to a church, standing isolated from any hamlet or houses near—a thing common in the country, but more particularly in Wales. We made directly up to it, and concealing ourselves in the gloom, we soon heard the voice of Gilbert, saying,—

"The storm was fortunate; you see their track is plain to be seen."

I now perceived how they had traced us. The soil being soft and chalky, and though only in half light armour, my steps left a strong impression. We passed rapidly round the church to try to find an opening, as their figures were plain to be seen at the extremity of the road, and if we attempted to emerge from the road, her white dress, and the gleam of my morion, must be seen. At length, by good fortune, we found a small door that led to the vaults under the church, and which had been probably left open to admit air, and forgotten by the sacristan. We entered instantly, and endeavoured to fasten it, but the bolt was on the outer side. Descending the flight of steps, we came into the vault. Light being admitted by two or three barred apertures, we could just see sufficient to conceal ourselves between a double row of coffins which were piled one upon the other, lying close to them. We heard them ride round the church; they paused at the aperture that was directly facing us.

"The steps go no further on the road," said one; "and 'tis impossible to trace them on the grass. Have they struck into the wood, or over the fields, or have they entered here?"

"We'll search, at all events," exclaimed the hated voice of Gilbert.

They dismounted—we trembled with anxiety; we heard their steps come up to the door, which we had pushed to as hard as we could; the wet having swelled the wood it stuck, and they had some little difficulty in pushing it open.

"This door is open," cried one.

"Yes," said the other; "but, by its sticking so confoundedly, cannot have been opened for some time; but let's see where it leads to."

Our hearts sank within us as we heard them descending.

"Stay," said Gilbert,—"what a horrid smell!—paugh! 'tis a vault! Let's get out of this; no woman could be got to enter a place like this, I am certain."

With that, to our inexpressible joy, we heard them go out and pull the door after them. They were a long time afterwards on the outside; and now, indeed, we felt the horrors of our situation. The effluvia from the dead bodies was overpowering, and the noise of the rats running over the coffins proved the quantity of them. Isabel clung to me in fear as she leaned her arm on the coffin behind us. One of them sprang upon it; a faint shriek appalled it and scared it hence, but filled us with alarm that it had been heard. The two men approached the barred aperture, and we saw them in the moonlight stand and listen. We scarcely dared to breathe. For a quarter of an hour did they thus keep watch—it appeared to us an age. At length the man I had seen so favoured by Beatrice grew impatient, and said,—

"I tell you it's only the squeal of a rat, and all's safe. If they have gone over the fields, if we ride hard we may yet meet them; but if we stay any longer here, we may as well give it up altogether;" with this they mounted their horses and rode off.

We still kept our position till some time after the sound of their horses' hoofs had faded on the ear. I then, to my alarm, found that Isabel was fainting; the pestiferous vapour had been too much for her, joined to the excitement of mind; but taking her to the aperture, the fresh air revived her a little. We then resolved to quit our horrid shelter, when what can paint our horror at finding the door fast— they had bolted it on the outside, top and bottom. This accounted for the remark of "All's safe" the impatient one had made use of. In vain we tried to shake the door or lift it from its hinges—it was immoveable; we were left to perish—buried quick with the dead. Embracing each other, we gave way to poignant grief, I cursing myself for having been the primitive cause of all.

At length an idea struck me; and though it promised but little hope, still something must be tried. I went to all the apertures and tried to move the bars, in hopes that some, corroded by time and the weather, might yield. I tried several, but to no purpose. But one now remained—it was the last hope of those who were indeed near hopeless. On trying the centre bar it moved, and though compelled to effect all with my left arm, I succeeded in wrenching it out. Using it as a lever, I succeeded with another at the side. The aperture was still insufficient to allow us to pass through, and the third bar seemed immovable. At length, exerting my whole strength and Isabel assisting, it broke in the centre. Still the ends had to be removed; but success so far cheered us, and using my dagger, I loosened the socket, where it was joined to the stone; the top piece fell out; and now, working with all the patience I possessed, in half an hour more I loosened the last bit. By the aid of the lever I now bent it, and the space seemed sufficient.

Isabel crept through first, when another difficulty presented itself. Though she could compress her form, and squeeze through, my armour completely prevented me from passing. I then, with much difficulty and her help, got it off, and leaving it there as a memento, I squeezed myself through, writhing in agony from the bruises and wounds that it set smarting afresh.

On our recovering our liberty, we for some time were obliged to sit and rest. The morning was now breaking fast; I knew not what way to take, nor the road our pursuers had taken; but proceeding at a venture, after walking about a mile, we overtook a hind, and with great joy learned that we had taken the right course, and were not far from Sir Edward's camp. This cheering us on, in less than two miles more the Castle of Rhys-ap-Howell met our view, and we presently reached my tent, where I was greeted by my companions in arms, who had feared I had been cut off by some party of the Welsh.

After taking refreshment, which was never more needed, I conveyed Isabel to a cottage, where some women belonging to the troops had taken up their abode, and who vied with each other in kind offices to her. I then had my own hurts looked to; my shoulder was dislocated, and a compound fracture appeared just above the elbow. I was covered with wounds and bruises innumerable. I was compelled to keep my couch for some days, during which time I obtained from Sir Edward the favour of a guard being put over the cottage where Isabel remained, so that I was sure of her safety.

It was on the third day of my confinement that, to my astonishment, Gilbert Brayle entered my tent and asked me for money. I now found by his discourse, that, not having seen me, he had no idea that I was the person that had rescued

Isabel. As I accused him of the fact at once, nothing could paint his astonishment to find that I was acquainted with the affair, which, however, he laid all to the boundless jealousy of his sister. As I was by no means inclined to parley with him, and was still smarting under the effects, I summoned the guard, and had him laid in chains, to be disposed of as Walter d'Arcy should decide.

The next day a truce was concluded between us and the Welsh—and a peace ultimately settled, their leader, Owen-ap-Cwr, being slain by Prince Richard in a skirmish. This Owen was the same white knight that bore off the palm at the passage-of-arms, in the tourney of Shrewsbury.

The army being now disbanded—as was the custom of those days, with the exception of such as were household or royal troops—I repaired to Shrewsbury, the place where the reduction took place, and a fever, in consequence of my late excitement, seizing me, Isabel would not leave me. I recovered in a much shorter space of time than was expected, during which time Gilbert had contrived to escape, and making his way to London, went to Walter d'Arcy's, and, with unparalleled effrontery, accused me of the abduction of Isabel, and gave notice of where we were, by which he got pardoned for his poaching offence, and a reward given to him by the deceived father.

As fate would have it, Isabel and I being so much together, she was in a fair way to be a mother before she was a wife. It was this prevented her from going to her parents till I was able to travel and go with her, and the difficulty of proving what I had asserted relative to the estate presenting itself to my mind, I was in no hurry to meet the storm. This was, however, all brought to a point by the sudden arrival of her father. Isabel fainted in my arms—the truth was impossible to be concealed, and Walter loaded me with abuse—accusing me of the abduction. In vain I attempted to speak. The appearance of Isabel seemed at once to corroborate all. Grown mad with rage, he drew his sword—for he had made inquiries at my father's, and was acquainted with that deceit too. Isabel, on her knees, implored him to be composed, and listen. His rage knew no bounds. And when, stung by his reproaches, I angrily bid him take his daughter and leave me, he made a lunge at me, just at the moment that she was rushing in between us, and ran his daughter through the heart.

Never shall I forget his cry of horror and despair as he threw himself upon the bed. For my own part, I rushed forth a maniac, and wandered I knew not where. What happened I know not. When I came to myself I was in a convent of Benedictine monks, in Northumberland. I had been found on the moor near the monastery, nearly naked, a most pitiable object. It was impossible to ascertain who I was or where I came from, my speeches were so incoherent. They had treated me with most Christian charity, and were much rejoiced when I returned to my reason. I found, on comparing the time with the period of Isabel's death, that near fourteen months had elapsed. On my acquainting them with who and what I was, they supplied me with clothes, a horse, and money, to be repaid when I was able. Taking an affectionate leave of the good monks, I arrived in due time in London, when, on repairing to my father's house, I found him just on the point of death. My brother had dropped dead suddenly by a rupture of a blood vessel, at the very time that the Welsh expedition had been disbanded at Shrewsbury, so that had I come up then, all might have gone smoothly, and Isabel now my happy wife. My father died the next day, and I came in for all his property, my sister having married a rich Spanish nobleman.

For some time after my father's death I kept myself secluded. Walter d'Arcy had lost his wife, and, stricken with grief, went abroad, throwing up his situation; which, to my astonishment, the villain Gilbert Brayle had got by dint of lying and shameless effrontery. Poor Walter wandered from country to country in sorrow, and was at length killed by the fall of an avalanche. From that time I became a very Nero or Caligula. There being a flaw in the marriage—indeed it was not known till after his death that he had been married at all—his children could not inherit—and indeed by law they would have but little—as the estate, which was my father's own acquiring, had never been left to Robert; nevertheless I always conceived that they would try to possess themselves of the property, and I took so great a dislike that I never would suffer them to come.

Some time after this I went over to Spain, and, London being hateful to me, now settled in Lisbon. The intrigue of the Spanish character suited me well. I had not been long there ere at church, one fast day, a sanctified duenna put a billet into my hand, and 1 afterwards saw her go to her charge, a lady, a most splendid figure of a woman, whose veil I had often wished in Eblis. The words ran to the effect, that if I was a man of equal gallantry and bravery as I was personal in appearance, and would be at the west corner of St. Pedro's church the evening of the next day, I might meet with an adventure that would probably turn out to my satisfaction. Of course there was no name to it. I was impatient till the time arrived.

I had since my arrival in Lisbon been introduced to a nobleman named Don Lopez de Castro, a man partial to the society of Englishmen, but insufferably proud, and though he honoured me by noticing me at the tavern, and on the Prado, he could by no means think of inviting a commoner to his table ; consequently, as I was as proud, we were not very friendly, and I felt a pleasure in mortifying his pride. I showed him the billet I received, maliciously observing how much the Spanish women thought of the Englishmen in preference to their own countrymen. He looked attentively at the billet, and I thought changed colour, and was evidently ill at ease all the evening, which I attributed to my jeering. The next night I was on the appointed spot, but enveloped in a large Spanish cloak and hat. As I walked to and fro, in thought, waiting for the appearance of the duenna, or some such emissary, I saw a figure standing in the shade of a porch, evidently watching me ; as I was convinced that no one could know me, enveloped as I was, and being acquainted with their mode of assassination, I immediately made towards the man to let him see that I was not to be taken by surprise, but before I reached the place where he stood, he darted further into the gloom of the cloister, until I lost all traces of him. Just at the same time I was pulled by the sleeve, and turning, beheld the duenna, who, enjoining me to be silent, led me to a street that was at the back of a row of the principal houses ; unlocking a garden-gate, we proceeded to an alcove, or summer-house, where I was charged to remain quite silent till her return ; she then left me. I then began to reflect on my own imprudence, as I might be murdered here, and nobody be any the wiser.

While thus cogitating, I heard voices, and presently a man and woman passed the summer-house, both muffled up in mantillas ; they spoke in a low key, but I could distinguish the words—" Spare not !" and " revenge !" I felt my situation anything but pleasant, but, grasping the hilt of my sword, I waited the result.

In a few moments the duenna made her appearance, and conducted me towards the house. I did not know whether to mention the circumstance of the man and woman to her or not—I judged them to be all in a league, but I was determined to see an end to the adventure. On entering the house I was shown up into a splendid chamber. I was then left to myself again ; in a few minutes she returned, and whispered to me that Donna Leonora would wait on me immediately, and that she herself was going to watch, lest the donna's husband should return. I was not more taken with the affair for that, but the duenna had scarcely left by one door, before my inamorato issued from another, armed, at all points for conquest. If I thought her figure charming, I thought her face beautiful.

Two hours fled like minutes in her fascinating society, when we were disturbed by Paquite, the duenna, who came in suddenly and whispered to her lady. I observed the colour of Leonora change, and she told me her husband was ascending the stairs. No time was to be lost ; I was led out by the other door, and hid in a closet in the passage. During the time I was there, I heard a man's voice in loud and angry speech in the chamber I had left, but the distance prevented me from distinguishing the words ; still I thought I knew the voice.

After a time Paquite released me from my confinement, and leading me to the garden-gate, appointed me to be there the next night at the same time. I returned to my hotel, pretty well satisfied with my adventure so far, and as the novelty pleased me, resolved, at least for a time, to continue it. In the morning, on the parade, I met Don Lopez, who fairly started as though he had seen a spectre, but collecting himself, apologised, and jokingly asked me about my adventure, which I recapitulated to him. He seemed shook by some strong emotion, but observing I noticed it, imputed it to indisposition. He asked me when I intended to repeat my visit. Mistrusting him, I answered carelessly, the same day in the next week ; and other merchants and hidalgos coming up, the subject dropped.

See page 61.

Faithful to my appointment, I was at the garden-gate at the exact time, and found Paquita waiting for me. I was soon in the presence of Leonora, who, in the course of our conversation, informed me that a famous cunning woman, or sorceress, had taken up her abode in Lisbon ; that she had been, like many others, tempted to visit her, and that the sorceress had told her she would soon have a lover from a distant land, and showed her his picture, which was the exact likeness of myself ;

that, on seeing me in the church, which I was in the habit of attending, she at once recognized the features, and believing that the affair was destined, she had been induced to make inquiries, and found that I was an Englishman, and so far fulfilling the description given by the cunning woman. She had scarcely gratified my curiosity by telling where the cunning woman was to be found, when Paquita entered, as pale as death, and besought Leonora to hide me somewhere, as her master was coming up the back stairs, and I could not go down the principal staircase without being seen by some of the servants, who were yet stirring. Leonora was at her wits' end, but at last thrust me into a cabinet that stood in a recess, curiously inlaid with mother-of-pearl, and made, apparently, to contain some figure or image, as it had no shelves. With some difficulty I squeezed myself into it, but a few seconds before the husband entered. As I could see through a crevice, I was anxious to ascertain what kind of personage the *cara sposa* was, whose voice I heard in no very gentle accents, and which, I was now convinced, was familiar to me. Guess my surprise when I found the husband to be no other than Don Lopez de Castro.

His singular behaviour was now explained. I had actually shown the wife's billet to the husband. He had thrown himself moodily on a Roman couch or settee, and was inveighing against her perfidy. Applying my ear to the crevice, I listened to his words.

"Yes, perjured woman," he cried, "you have deceived me; the poison was not given!"

In tears, she answered that I had, by accident, let fall the goblet, and thus frustrated the attempt; and then, with many protestations, asserted her innocence, and that I had left the casino unsatisfied.

"This shall be proved," he cried, "when the English villain returns to his appointment on Thursday. If he adheres to his word, in this apartment he dies; should he not come, I shall be convinced you have warned him, and are guilty; and, by the sacred cross, the fate intended for him shall be yours. Mark that, base woman! for, by all the saints above, as I have spoken so will I act."

He then rose and left the apartment. Leonora sat in tears some time, and I knew not whether to emerge from my hiding place, or whether she expected his immediate return.

After some time passed in disagreeable suspense, and in a most unpleasant position, being cramped by the awkward posture I was forced to stand in, Paquita entered, and having spoken to her mistress for a few minutes, they released me from my prison. They then informed me that Don Lopez had retired to his chamber, but that he had previously locked all the doors, and had taken the keys with him, thus preventing my entrance, having still doubts as to whether I had told him the truth.

On questioning her about the poison, she told me that after I had been so unthinking as to show him the billet, he had come home, and, in his rage, threatened to kill her, making her promise, as the only way to save her life, that when I came she would poison me. He mixed the fatal potion with his own hand, and left it against my arrival, which she threw away; but, forgetting to caution me, she had, when he came home, told him that I had drunk the wine, and complaining of indisposition, I had suddenly quitted.

Exulting in the success of his stratagem, and knowing that, from the subtle nature of the draught, I must perish, he had gone forth the next morning, assured that he should hear of my death. Hence his astonishment in beholding me. He had returned home in a violent rage, and it had put all her art to the test to pacify him, and save her own life; she had been fearful, the previous night of telling me of the affair, lest I should return no more; but she had intended to have warned me to keep out of his company.

Paquita having given me the exact address, and the mode of obtaining an audience of Signora Ilferoza, the sorceress, we now began to consult how I was to make my escape. The windows of the apartment I was in were a considerable height from the ground, but intervening was a sort of terrace, that went round the house, about four feet in breadth, and defended or fenced with parapets, giving it the appearance of a castellated mansion. To the terrace it was at least thirteen feet; and a large Cachmere shawl of Leonora's being produced, one end was made fast to the leg of a heavy table, and, holding to it, I attempted to slip down, but when at the end, was obliged to drop and fall upon the terrace. The fall, though but trifling, made me remember my precipitate passage through the trap in Wales; and my shoulder, which ever was troublesome, pained me excessively. Getting up, I made my way to the steps which led into the grounds, when suddenly voices arrested my attention. Looking over the parapet, I saw two men, apparently domestics, armed and keeping watch. From the position they were in, they could not see my descent, and, fortunately, they had not heard my fall.

"I tell you," says one, "Don Lopez is only giving us a good deal of trouble to no purpose. The gallant would hardly come a night like this."

"Confound him," says the other, "I only wish I could come across him; he should feel this," taking a pole-axe from his shoulder.

"Well," says the other, "I shall sit myself down."

With that he sat down on the very steps I had to descend, his companion taking his place by his side. I was completely blockaded; I walked round, but could find no other descent, and had given myself up, when, after pausing some time, I plainly heard one of the lacqueys snoring. On approaching them gently, the moon, fortunately, being obscured, I discovered that they were both asleep. I formed the bold determination of stepping over them, in doing which I caught my foot in the cloak of one of the men, and half awoke him; he growled a curse on the other, saying,—

"A murrain to you! Is not one cloak enough for you?"

I then stood straddling across him; had he looked up or opened his eyes, he must have seen me; but pulling the skirt of the cloak over his face, in a second or two he was oblivious again. I now got clear into the garden, but in a different part to that which I had been in. I knew I must scale the wall, which, near the garden gate, was low, and the trees growing near it, would assist me on the inside to gain the summit of the wall, from whence I must either jump or let myself down into the street.

Taking the direction which I thought most likely to lead to the alcove, I proceeded at a smart pace, when suddenly I heard the deep bay of a hound close to me. In the light, I then saw a large black dog, of the Spanish bloodhound species, making its way across the lawn directly towards me. Quickening my pace into a run, I fortunately came to the alcove, and directly made for the wall. The animal was within a yard of me. I caught hold of the branch of a tree, and swung myself on to the top, but not quick enough to prevent the beast from seizing my cloak, from which he tore a large piece. When on the wall, the leap into the street was inconsiderable, and soon effected. I had now cleared the premises, but was not out of danger yet, for I was stopped by the night-watch, who paraded the town in pairs. These two men demanded to know who I was, and what I had been doing on the premises of Don Lopez—threatening, on my hesitating, to take me before the corregidor. Having heard the character of the city-watch before, I offered them money, telling them that I had been to see my sweetheart, an abigail in the don's service; and I was suffered to pursue my way without further molestation, though remarking that they should hear in the morning if anything was wrong, and that they should be sure to find me out.

When I lay down on my couch, my thoughts ran on the sorceress, and her producing my picture. I remembered having one taken of me when I was first acquainted with the Brayles, considered to be too old a likeness, and cast aside among the lumber; and in my first excess of passion for Beatrice, I had taken, clandestinely, out of our house and presented her, for which I was reprimanded by my father, who said that, in time, it would be a faithful resemblance, though not at the present. That picture had no doubt been seized at the time their cottage was sold; and I was anxious to know in what manner it had fallen into the hands of the sorceress.

The next evening, when it became dusk, I sought the part of the town that Paquita had described, and in an obscure street found the house she mentioned; it was old-fashioned, mean, and dilapidated.

Giving three single knocks, I was surprised to see a black round ball of a head thrust through a wicket in the door, about three feet from the ground, which addressed me in French,—

"Qui va la?"

Remembering my instructions, I answered,—

"De Castro, vive Ilferoza" (faith and confidence).

The door then seemed to open of its own accord, and I entered a smoke-dried, dirty, dark passage, lit up by a rude lamp that blackened the roof with the smoke, and hardly made darkness visible. The door closed after me with a crash that made me start and look round, when I saw standing behind it a black dwarf, less than four feet high, whose ears, protruding from the head, gave him a most fiend-like look; his eyes, too, were unusually large, and the two front teeth projected over his under lip. He was dreadfully deformed, being hunchbacked and bow-legged; his feet were of an immense size, turned inwards, which made his walk more like the shuffling pace of a bear than the step of a human being. In silence he stood till I requested to see the signora, and put a piece of money in his hand, on which his features assumed something resembling a grin; and, ascending a flight of stairs, he ushered me into a large room hung with black, and pointing to a seat, disappeared behind some arras at the end of the apartment, which I had now an opportunity of examining.

Several skeletons were hanging from the roof; they consisted of those of two human beings, a crocodile, a wolf, an eagle or vulture, with the head of a shark. On a table, which was covered with a crimson cloth, with black and white hieroglyphics, stood two globes and an hour-glass; the dried hand of a mummy, secured to a block of wood, held a torch, composed of some material which cast a red glare around the apartment; two human skulls also graced the board, and a large black cat, which rose at my entrance, but afterwards resumed its place. Several books were lying open, but in such old-fashioned characters that it would have required some learned pundit or gifted antiquarian to decipher them.

After some time spent in waiting, which I could see was to weaken the mind by the sight of the horrible objects around, a tall woman, in black flowing robes, entered, her head covered by a coif, or head-dress of a nun. Her face was pale, though little could be seen of it; she advanced to a seat at the table, and from two small cabinets, one at each end of the table, two enormous toads came crawling out, as if to meet her, and sat in the centre, with the cat between them, the eyes of the precious triumvirate being fixed upon the visitor.

"What seeks John Beauchamp, the Englishman, of the Spanish sorceress?" said the woman, in a voice that startled me. But assuming a stern tone and manner, I exclaimed,—

"It appears I am known to you, but I am not to be wrought upon by this ridiculous display. I came here to ask a question, and demand a straightforward reply. How came my picture in your possession, and what was your motive in making use of it as you have done? I will acquaint the corregidor, and have you punished as your offences deserve, in deluding the unwary."

"And were all punished as they deserve for deluding the unwary, what would be the fate of the murderer of Isabel D'Arcy?" she replied.

I started from my seat in astonishment, and cold drops of perspiration stood on my brow.

"Who and what are you, woman?" I exclaimed.

"Your superior," she cried; "for I can make you tremble. Respect my power, or beware of the effects."

"I am not to be juggled with," I exclaimed; "and, by hell, you either answer my questions, or I will drag you this instant before the tribunal," at the same time drawing my sword, and holding it to her throat.

Far from being intimidated, she answered by a scornful laugh; and, stamping with her foot, the arras was lifted, and four bravoes, with drawn weapons, entered the apartment, and surrounded me.

The skeletons seemed to shake and move in antic dance; the eyes of all the skulls gleamed with meteoric fire; the black cat rose, and arching her huge back, seemed on the point of flying at me, while the toads, and a large snake I had not before observed, kept a continual motion on the table.

"You see," she exclaimed, "that I am not unprotected. Another word of insolence, and you die; but amend the past, keep former promises inviolate, and I yet may be your friend."

Amazed and confounded, I cried,—

"Inexplicable being, what mean you?—what promises?—when made, and to whom?"

"To her whom you have wronged," she cried, stamping her foot, on which her myrmidons retired as instantaneously as they had appeared. "Have you no remembrance," she said, removing part of the shroud-like covering of her face, "of Beatrice Brayle?"

It was, indeed, that singular woman who stood before me. I staggered.

"Beatrice!" I exclaimed.

"Ay," she said, "and your bitter enemy; but, the idol removed, let the past be forgotten."

So saying, she extended her hand; mechanically I took it, though my heart revolted, and my blood chilled at the touch of the being to whom I ever attributed the loss of Isabel.

"What means this?" I faintly uttered.

"That I have ever sought to be revenged, and attained one part of my desire—another day, and I had completed my aim. But even in the heart of the most depraved, first love hath power. I see you are willing to forget the past; let us both bury it in oblivion. I am able to become your friend, and increase your fortune. If avarice, if ambition be your darling aim, your ruling passion, I can gratify it, on your solemn promise that on your quitting this country, or on your stay, in one year from this day you make me your wife; otherwise," she cried, "behold!" lighting a taper composed of dead men's fat, and other horrid ingredients, as I afterwards was made acquainted with, "as this wastes,"—and pointing to the numerous circles of its coil, "'twill last," she said, "full many a day—as this wastes so shall you, and when it expires, so shall the vital spark expire in you."

Surprised, subdued, even alarmed at this fearful woman, I took an oath equivocal (for I meant not its performance,) that I would wed her at the time appointed. Not content with the mere words, she made me wish the torments of purgatory to be my portion for ever, if I kept it not, and that I might die in horrors, unshrived, unheard, unaided, hated, detested and accursed. She then, taking a piece of parchment composed of dead men's skin, she opened a vein in her arm with a dagger, and then wrote down the words of the contract or vow. Then taking my hand, unmanned and passive from superstitious dread as I had become, she slightly wounded my wrist—it still bears the mark, you see, raising the sleeve of his dress—and dipping a pen in it, made me sign it in the same manner as she had done. This ceremony performed, she told me that she had retained the picture since I gave it to her, that after I saw her in Wales, she left Britain with a knight of the Teutonic order, who was afterwards executed for his crimes at Rome. She then joined a Zingaro tribe, and got initiated in all the mysteries of their art so deeply, that she quitted them, and set up for herself in fortune-telling and the black art. That meeting with a monk of Lyons, named Father Amboise, who had made magic and the occult sciences his study, instead of the bible and psalter, she became his wife, and they repaired to Lisbon, where they were both practising on the credulity of the people. They had been to Vienna, Paris, Naples, and Madrid, and their gains were immense; but she hated him, and truly believed that he was in league with fiends, for his power exceeded all human art. That the only being who had a hold of him was herself, as she could at any time bring him to the rack and stake. That he knew by his art the hour in which he should quit the world, which he had told her would be on such a day, in such a month. The period was now close at hand. She was compelled to remain unmarried for twelve lunar months, the year of the calendar completing the time of his life and her probation. I should then become possessed of all his wealth. That she had heard of my arrival in Lisbon, and knowing Don Lopez to be a most jealous and revengeful character, ever consulting her power to discover his wife's gallants, when Leonora came to her, whose turn for intrigue had also been communicated by her spies, she showed her my picture, and worked upon her amorous disposition to send for me, at the same time that she, Beatrice, gave notice to the husband, that he might take my life. It was she who passed the door of the alcove with him the first night I went to Leonora's; but Paquita had managed the affair so secretly, that she did not know of my being there till the next day. It was she, too, that had provided the poison Don Lopez gave to his wife for me, one drop of which, she said, would have destroyed me on the instant, the composition of it being one of her greatest secrets, and possessed but by two more in the world. I shuddered when I thought of the power of this terrible woman, and the risk that I had run. When I asked her why she did not have me stabbed by one of her bravoes, instead of taking so complicated a course, as I was easy to have been taken off that way at any time she said that Don Lopez had offended her, by accusing her husband to the archbishop, and Leonora had jeered her, and affected to despise her power; therefore, she said, I thought to have my revenge complete, by making you the destruction of each other.

On asking her how she came to change her sentiments so completely in regard to myself, she said she had seen me on the prado; that her heart acknowledged its first affection, and that it was her intention to send to me and effect an interview. She then threw her arms around my neck, and fear made me return her caresses. She gave me a superb diamond buckle, and a bag of gold, but told me my intimacy with Leonora must now cease; that I must send to the donna to say, that fearing I should be the means of her husband taking her life or otherwise ill-treating her, I, as a gentleman, begged leave to decline prosecuting the affair any further. This Beatrice insisted on, as also my continence with regard to any other woman. "Remember," she cried, "no more Isabels." Had I not disliked her before, I should have done so for making use of that name so slightingly; but at the time I thought that silence was my best course. She told me she should introduce me to the monk Amboise, her husband, as a near relative and valued friend. At my smiling at the idea of a married monk, she laughed, and said, "Better that than a life of celibacy, which was one of hypocrisy, dissembling, and vice. The holy father was no worse than his brethren, but even better, since, though he broke one oath, he had taken another." Then acquainting me with her residence, this being only the scene of her professional pursuits, she embraced me again, and we parted.

On my return to my hotel, I sought in sleep to drown the memory of the last few hours' events. I obeyed the request of Beatrice, relative to Leonora; at the same time I had no particular wish to be always in dread of a jealous husband's dagger; I was satisfied with so far of the adventure, and begged to decline further proceedings. When I met Don Lopez, he questioned me as to my intrigue, when I feigned to have had a letter from my sister, which had so painted the miseries attendant upon intrigues in married life in so lively a manner, that having found my inamorata to be a wedded wife, I had given up the pursuit, acting up to the Christian precept of doing to others as I would they did to me. On this Don Lopez arose, and embraced me for my good Catholic feelings, as he termed it, never letting it appear that he was the husband, or even acquainted with Leonora. I thought then that I had washed my hands of the affair, but I was still to answer it, as will appear in the sequel.

> " The moments fly,
> And time flits by,
> Like swallows on the wing,
> But follies past
> Too oft at last
> Eternal sorrows bring."

Paquita, the duenna, made several efforts to see me, but in order to save myself from her assiduities, I changed my place of residence to an hostel at the opposite quarter of Lisbon. According to promise, I was introduced by Beatrice to her ghostly husband, with whom I soon got so friendly, he having no idea of the real connection between Beatrice and myself, that he revealed all the impostures of the monks of his order, among which were some of the vilest that were ever practised on the credulity of mankind. The blood of our Saviour preserved in a phial, consisting of some chemical preparation, that always remained in a fluid state, but yet so turgid in its course, as never to let more than a drop escape at a time. He was the head machinist of the holy fathers' impostures. By his contrivance, a figure of our Saviour, as large as life, nailed to the cross, shed tears continually for the crimes of mankind. The head was hollow, and affixed over an opening in the wall. Two small tin cups were put at the back of the eyes, sloping downwards a little. A small slit was made under the eye-balls, which were directly on a parallel with the surface of the water in the cups. A quantity of very small fish, or fry of fish, was put into the cups, which kept continually swimming about, and agitating the water, which trickled out at the opening under the eyes, by a drop at a time, thus giving the exact appearance of the image crying *bona-fide* tears. His raising the dead, and curing the sick, were infamous impositions, but clever, and to the ignorant marvellous indeed.

Some of the monk's devices being seen through by a rival practitioner, the holy charlatan was denounced, and cited to appear before the sacred tribunal, as the inquisition, then in its infancy, or beginning, was termed. Aware of its severity, he kept for a time concealed until a favourable opportunity occurred for escaping to Italy.

In the interim, Donna Leonora, being offended at the slight I had put upon her, resolved to be revenged; and what will not a jealous or offended woman stick at? Once slight their affection, their pride takes the alarm, and the object of love is now made the object of hate. She informed Don Lopez of the whole affair from beginning to end, even swearing to meetings since the night of my escaping from the window, so that he resolved to take me off by murder in some way; but assassinations having been of too frequent occurrence, the government were exceedingly vigilant, so that he resolved to take me off by poison, as originally intended, and came to Beatrice to provide him some as before, which she did, being munificently rewarded for it; she, at the same time, told me of the affair, warning me to be guarded.

Pretending increasing friendship for me, Lopez invited me to his house. It was some time before I cared for entering the well-known premises, but being resolved to see an end to the adventure, I went. Our meeting was strictly private, and a handsome collation was served up. He apologized for the non-appearance of his lady, by saying his whole family were gone on a water excursion on the Tagus with his brother-in-law, which I knew to be false, as I had heard Leonora's voice as I ascended the principal flight of stairs; I, however, took no notice of it; Paquita attended as governante, and did the honours of the table. I had been liberal to her in my visits to the house, and it appears that now she was not ungrateful, though her mistress, in conjunction with her husband, sought my life. When we were seated to our wine, two massy gold goblets, of exquisite workmanship, and great value, were placed before us, both of the same pattern. Paquita, then, under pretence of wiping some dust from my goblet, but, in reality, in obedience to the private signal of her master, while thus ostensibly employed, she emptied a liquid from a small phial into the goblet; in the gleam of the precious metal it was not seen, and she replaced it before me, Don Lopez on the instant filling it to the brim with some rare wine, which he had been previously extolling. As I before mentioned, he was partial to England and the British, and I engaged him in close conversation, contriving to direct his attention to an object to be seen from the window, to exemplify my discourse. While I thus stood with him at the window, Paquita, who had sent the lacqueys for more wine, and given the keys to them, now in an instant changed the goblets, both equally filled, and we returned to our seats. Don Lopez pledged me, and drained his goblet to the dregs, challenging me to do the same, a custom in that country, which, when I imitated, his satisfaction was evident. He could scarce contain himself, unconscious that he was rejoicing at his own downfall. At as early a period as I could, and making a pretext of urgent business the next morning, I left the don, whose countenance and eyes began to denote the influence of the fatal draught, and I wished not to be present at the time of his death, lest I should be implicated. In a few hours he died, raving on Leonora, St. Ilferoza, and myself. On his death she sent to me by Paquita, whom I rewarded handsomely for her valuable aid; but returned an evasive answer to her mistress, which so enraged her, that she denounced me to the Tribunal. I was, therefore, compelled to fly with Amboise and Beatrice, who was also denounced for her fortune-telling. In the dead of the night, then, we made our way from the place of our concealment to the water side; our property was already on board a vessel belonging to the Italian states, and was then lying in the river ready to sail, the wind being fair, and the good ship but waiting for us, its living freight; but we had yet some risk to incur. Pedro, the brother to Don Lopez, had sworn to revenge his brother's death on me; for that purpose he hired bravos, and watched for me at my usual haunts. As we were taking a near turning to also avoid the frequented part of the quay, Gobold, the black dwarf, who also accompanied us, gave notice of the men lurking in the shade, apparently waiting to waylay us. Amboise, who had laid aside his monastic habit, now drew his sword, as I did also, and Beatrice, arming herself with a long sharp stiletto, we waited patiently for the advance of the villains.

We directly after saw them emerge from their hiding-place, in number, four, with one who appeared to be their leader, whom Beatrice instantly recognised as Don Pedro, the brother of Lopez.

"Villains, murderers!" he cried, "take the reward of your villany!"

They then made a rush at us. I parried the thrusts of Pedro, and one of the bravos; Amboise engaged two more; and Beatrice, seeing the disadvantage of the odds, seized the fourth bravo, and struggled with him, till, seeing her opportunity, she thrust the stiletto into his heart; Gobold, the dwarf, got between the legs of one of the men engaged with Amboise, and threw him down, then leaping upon his chest, pinned him to the ground. With my two adversaries I was not so fortunate; they were evidently better swordsmen than myself, and the mask that he had assumed, falling from Pedro's face, his features in the light of the moon bore so strong a resemblance to Lopez, (who, though he deserved his fate, I felt I had injured) that it partly unnerved me. Fortunately Amboise succeeded in disarming and mortally wounding his antagonist, and came to my assistance, Beatrice and Gobold being engaged in binding the overpowered. Still we found our hands full, and were saved by the timely arrival with the boat from the ship, when Pedro, fearing detection, fled with his remaining adherent; as we had no wish to make prisoners, we left the men to shift for themselves, and remove the dead body; while we, jumping into the boat, soon got alongside of the Zephyr, which set sail immediately.

Since that time, after our arrival in Florence, the place of our destination, Amboise, as he had prophesied, took ill, and it was evident that his end was near; he refused all medical aid, or the assistance of a priest; he raved incessantly, and the night of his death was most terrific—one of the greatest storms I ever witnessed; sheets of lightning illumined the deathbed, and the awful thunderclap drowned the groans of the dying man. His hair, which he suffered to grow, stood on end with horror; his eyes seemed darting from their sockets. Grasping the hand of Beatrice, and my arm, he implored of us not to leave him; then, starting up, entreated the door to be fastened.

"Shut it—bolt it—keep him!" he cried, in wild frenzy. "Ha! the window—fast—fast—make it fast. Hold the doors firm—do not leave me. Beatrice, remember your vow. My will is in the cabinet—the original in the Chancery of Padua. You lose all—all—should you wed before ——. Ha, ha! See—see—

the door opens—that face—that eye. Mercy—mercy. Oh, save the wretched soul of ——"

Blood gushed now in torrents from throat, ears, nose, and eyes. He had broken a blood vessel in his dreadful struggle, and he expired with the bitterest groan I ever heard. In less than an hour afterwards his whole form turned black, and he was obliged to be buried the night following. This singular occurrence, his

refusal to see either leech or priest, and the men that put him into the coffin remarking the appearance of the corse was uncommon, an inquiry was set on foot, and the deceased being reported to be rich, we were cited to appear before the council, which, not suiting our views, we escaped again in the night, and sailed for Genoa. Here we remained some time, till Beatrice began to talk about the marriage. I could not endure the idea of wedding such a creature, and resolved, at all hazards, to avoid so horrible a tie, despite my oath. We then mutually

commenced our plans unknown to each other.   On various pretexts I contrived
to get the money of Amboise placed in such foreign money-holders' hands in my
name, and having secured such diamonds and valuables as I was able in the time,
I got all my property on board a ship in the harbour, and made up my mind to
leave Genoa and Beatrice, and set sail for England.

The night previous I observed Beatrice unusually melancholy, and endeavoured
to rally her out of it.   We lived in a splendid palazzo, I had hired during our
stay ; for Beatrice lived in the utmost style of extravagance, and insisted on my
taking the appellation of Count Montaldi, herself the countess, our household
and suite corresponding in all points with our self-created patent letter of
nobility.   We kept a great deal of company, but on the night in question,
except at the commencement, had but few.   When they had retired, and we
were in our chamber it was that I made the remark before mentioned.   Beatrice
complained of indisposition ; I said I hoped that Ribalto, our major-domo, would
look to the doors.

"Every door is locked," she said, in a most emphatic manner.   "I have looked
to that."

I thought her manner exceedingly odd ; she had never looked to the locking of
the gates and doors before.   I asked her if she was going to the margrave's ball
the next evening.

"Where shall you be to-morrow evening?" she cried, [fixing her large full
eyes on the ground.

"Heaven knows where I may be to-morrow evening."

She afterwards kept a moody silence, and wearied with my useless attempts to
make her conversant, I fell asleep.   I was awoke by the smell of fire—starting
up, I saw that Beatrice still sat in the same position, her eyes fixed with a horrid
glare on me.

"Good God !" I exclaimed, "what is the matter, and wherefore do you gaze
on me thus ?   The palazzo is surely on fire !"

"It is on fire," she exclaimed, "and you must perish with me !   I have
placed combustibles and compositions, taught me by Amboise, in certain places,
all to ignite at a fixed period ; I have discharged the household, have locked
every door, and thrown the keys into the river.   One alone will know the story
of our fate, and will reveal the cause," was the reply, in a voice that startled me.
"He now watches the fire, and should it fail, would renew it in every quarter.
Hark ! do you hear the roar of the flames ?   the shouts of the multitude ?
Perjured villain, I am acquainted with your plans, have watched you at every
turn !   If you will not wed me, you shall perish with me, for here we die
together !"

Horrorstruck I rushed to the window—the scene was tremendous ; the burning palazzo cast a red glare on the faces of thousands of spectators, who were
gazing on the vast conflagration.   There had evidently been measures taken to
prevent all aid ; and the water was so near, yet little or no exertion was made to
save the building ; a part of the roof falling outwards, took a large portion of the
front with it, disclosing us to the view of the populace.   Shouts and cries announced their horror and indignation, for they saw that she detained me forcibly
in the room.   At this moment a flight of stairs that led to the private chambers
of the officers of the palazzo, struck me as being attainable, and if to be reached
would probably be the means of saving my life.   I sprang to the door, and with
the frenzy of a man at the point of death, forced it open.   She still clang to me ;
the centre of the roof had fallen in, and the main interior looked like an immense
crater of flame.   The part of the palazzo we were in, being supported by large
iron pillars, sustained that portion of its roof, and being chiefly stone, baffled
the fury of the flames for some time.

"No, villain !" cried Beatrice, "we part not !   In life and death you are
mine !"

At that time I had dragged her to the end of the gallery, when to my horror I
found a portion of the stairs had fallen in, and to the place I wanted to reach it

would take a very active leap. It was, however, no time to pause; Beatrice saw my design in my eye, and clasping her arms together round me, she cried,—

"No, no, we part not. You cannot leap the distance with me hanging round your neck, and I rejoice that I am the weight that pulls you down. It is not love now, but hate, that urges me. You have slighted—deceived me! I now destroy you!"

The heat of the flames now was insupportable; mad—infuriated, I tore her arms from my body, and hurled her from me. She sprang to me again, but in the moment intervening I had drawn my sword; she sprang upon its point, and it entered her heart. I still see her look as she fell. On the instant I had cleared the gulph, and stood on the safe part, as it seemed, for a few minutes. I was again visible to the people; they cheered me, and ladders were applied, yet not long enough to reach the place; they called on me to jump, and all held their cloaks. I dared not, and yet dared not remain. Ropes were thrown by some mechanic force, and one reached me. I caught hold of it, and made it fast to the window-bar.

The palazzos of Genoa are built in the Norman style, of an immense height, multiplying the suites of chambers. The rope was slender, the distance full eighty feet from the ground. I was warned the roof was falling, and I put one foot out of the window, holding the rope. The action was perceived; ladders were quickly braced, and applied, but nearly twenty feet short of my reach. Carpets were extended below; an adventurous soldier mounted the ladder, and I began my descent; the mob gazed in breathless anxiety; the soldier stood on the last ring of the ladder; I was within two yards of him; the rope broke, he caught at me, and was overbalanced—we both fell into the carpet extended below. The shouts of the crowd were deafening. With the exception of some contusions we were both safe, and taken to the nearest house, where we were attended to with the tenderest care; but I was insensible, and did not recover my senses for some days.

When I came to myself I found that the body of Beatrice had been found almost a perfect cinder. It was supposed that she had attempted to follow me and had been suffocated by the smoke, thus falling a victim to the flames. My guilt was not known; the vessel, having been solely engaged by myself, still remained in the harbour, and as soon as my strength permitted I repaired on board, after having liberally rewarded the gallant soldier. We set sail, and not till we were out of sight of land did I recover my composure of mind.

On the first night we were out I was sitting at the door of my cabin on deck— the watch were asleep on their post, and the very helmsman having fastened the tiller, nodded drowsily over it; we were becalmed. While thinking of the late dreadful event, a black figure emerged from the hold, and startled me. It was Gobolt, the dwarf; he had concealed himself in the vessel, and stood insultingly before me.

"Signor, count," he cried, "we have had a near risk of it! I was in the burning palazzo myself till after you quitted it. I saw you slay my mistress—I could have saved you then, but in revenge left you to your fate. I have concealed myself in the vessel to punish you. The captain must take me to England, when I will denounce you. Though you did not, I loved my mistress. Who but she would have been kind to the poor deformed negro? You shall not escape the hands of justice."

Enraged, I seized the wretched abortion. In vain he struggled; he was as a fly in my grasp, and I bore him to the side of the vessel. He saw my design; with his large rolling eyes extended beyond their sockets; in fear, he begged of me to spare him, in the greatest terror; but his threat chilled my heart, and his prayer was unheeded. He shrieked, and I plunged his carcase in the wave. A shark, who had been playing in the moonbeams by the side of the vessel, saw him, his silver belly glanced as he turned on his back like a flash of lightning, and in less than a second the wretched negro was bit in two, and sank with the scaly monster. His death shriek had roused the men; they inquired the cause, and

I attributed it to myself, and my terrors at seeing so many of those monsters of the deep about the ship, for a shoal of them seemed to sport round the vessel. The men laughed at my fears, and returned to their duty, and I to my berth, but not to sleep. Another murder had been added to the catalogue of my crimes.

We arrived safely in port; having in vain attempted to lose reflection in the society of the dissipated, I at length entered the monastery of St. Mark Han, at Stonar, becoming a monk, and endowing the convent with my ill-gotten treasure.

CHAPTER V.

THE monk Urban having finished his narrative, they returned to the convent, Albert shuddering to think of the crimes of the wretch he had selected as his friend; yet Albert was a wretch as base as himself. On what trifling events does our future fate depend. Had either of those men taken a different course when the first difficulty of life presented itself, how different had been their lot.

The next day Albert, in roving through the wood, saw a lady, attended by a retainer, enter the cottage of a wood-cutter. He bowed when she passed him, but so different was he in appearance to what he was when she last beheld him, that Sabina (for it was she), knew him not. Rooted to the spot he remained gazing on her as she entered the cottage. After a short time the retainer issued from it, apparently sent back to the castle for some purpose; Albert accosted him, and, pretending to be walking the same way, entered into converse with him. He said that the woodman's child was ill, so ill that little hope remained of his life—that the Lady Sabina had herself, for three nights, sat at its pallet, attending to its wants. The woodman's wife had lately been delivered of twins, and was herself unable to look to her dying first-born. The father was inconsolable. The paternal feelings are more tremblingly alive to the first child than any of those that follow—at least in its days of infancy. He was now despatched to the castle to fetch a skilful leech, one of the baron's household. Under pretence of not detaining the man on his charitable errand, Albert paused, and he rode on.

When left to himself, Albert again turned his steps towards the cottage. Some trees stood before its window, and, concealing himself behind the trunk of one, he had an opportunity of viewing the interior. It was a wretched cabin, consisting but of one apartment; in a corner was the bed of the mother and twins, seemingly made comfortable by coverings from the castle, on the other side of the fireplace was the pallet of the child, a little attenuated creature that seemed to breathe with difficulty, and whose eyes were fixed upon its mother, who, sitting up in her own bed, looked with streaming eyes on her darling boy. Sabina knelt by its side, endeavouring to coax it to take a spoonful of some rich conserve she held in her hand; but nature refused; and the father, who sat with clasped hands in the middle of the room, seemingly shook his head in token that all was nearly over.

Moved by the scene, but still more with a view of ingratiating himself with Sabina, he entered the cottage, the dress of the noviciate being his introduction. The woodman rose and bowed as Albert pronounced the accustomed "benedicite;" Sabina looked up and made a slight obeisance, but tears nearly blinded her, and she knew him not. He knelt by the side of her and prayed over the dying child, the voice of Sabina joining frequently in the holy duty. While thus employed the retainer, at full speed, returned with the leech, who, entering immediately, took the hand of the patient. He felt his feeble pulse, and all eyes were directed to him; no hope was in his look. The mother first broke silence: a motion from the leech stayed further question. The dying boy seemed to struggle, the lower jaw was convulsed, its little arms were extended to its maternal parent, the eyes closed, then opened, a deep sigh burst from its little chest, and the eyes closed for ever. The shriek of the mother was appalling, the father sprang towards her; Sabina, overpowered, had sunk but for

Albert's arm; the leech clasped his hands in grief, and even the retainer's cheeks were wet with tears.

When the first emotion had somewhat subsided, the leech and retainer entreated Sabina to return to Richborough, nor suffer the event to affect her health and spirits, in which Albert ventured to join; but Sabina sympathised too much with the sufferings of the parents to think of herself; but Albert having observed that sorrow was sacred, and delighted in solitude, where none could see it, she reluctantly complied. At this time it was Albert whispered his name to her; she changed colour and started, but, retaining her mind, she gave her hand with a faint smile of recognition.

Having said a few kind words to the distressed couple, and leaving them some money to defray the necessary expenses, she took the arm of Albert, desired the two men to proceed to the castle with the horses, as she should walk through the wood attended by the holy brother; fortunately Albert was not known to either. On the horses being out of earshot, Sabina told him that if seen near the castle it would cost him his life; even after he had assumed the cowl it would be dangerous to approach its precincts. She repressed every allusion to love, and finally extinguished hope by telling him that, if her father was dead, she should as strictly forbid him the castle herself. In vain he told her he was a being new created; that not the robber captain, but the fugitive soldier stood before her.

"'Tis useless," said Sabina, "to urge that which I must not hear. I gave a promise to my father so solemn—a promise exacted by reason and gratitude—that I never would become yours; that promise has been given but three days, but never shall be broken. As a friend, as a brother, I shall ever look upon you, will ever serve you; but remember, if you, regardless of this injunction, ever breathe a word on the subject of our former childish passion, we meet no more."

Albert would have spoken, but the stern, haughty look and carriage of Sabina, proving her a true scion of the Norman Fitzormond, froze his hopes and fettered his tongue. In silence they had gained the centre of the little wood that divided Richborough from the Stonar boundary, and she, withdrawing her arm, requested him to return, hinting at the possibility of their meeting the baron. Albert implored her to let him see her again; she consented, when he should have become a monk, and buried all sublunary feelings, when a pure and sacred friendship might be entertained, that no time could cool or changes alter. Giving him her hand, with one of those smiles that fascinated all who saw them, she left him, and tripping up the avenue of trees was quickly out of sight; the castle turrets o'ertopping the leafy denizens of the wood denoting its proximity. More in love than ever, bereft of every hope, and shrinkingly conscious of his own unworthiness, he retraced his steps through the wood, his head sunk on his bosom and his arms folded in sorrow's knot.

Deeply ruminating, he knew not that he was noted by one whose penetrating eye saw quickly into the state of his mind. The being alluded to was an old woman well known as the Witch of the Wood, a sibyl who, like the famous hag of Endor and the no less famous Shipton, dealt in charms and prophecies, some of which had chanced to be fulfilled so truly that she was sought by the idle, the wicked, and the credulous, in crowds from all parts to consult her. She had been engaged in the witch's occupation from time immemorial of picking sticks, and, as Albert advanced, she rested her bundle on the trunk of a fallen tree, and in a hollow voice thus addressed him,—

> "Man of woe, go seek the land;
>   Strive thy form and soul to save.
> Man of woe, avoid the strand;
>   Demons lurk within the wave."

Albert started at the words, but recognising the sybil, he took a coin from his gypsine and holding it to her tried to pass.

"I want no money; I would warn thee, if I could. Last night I saw thy planet near the moon; blood red it shone, surrounded by black and fearful clouds; a drop fell from it, I caught it ere it reached the earth and put it in the charmed well, and in the vapour that arose I read thy fate. I may not tell all; but that which I tell is true.

> " Man of woe, go seek the land;
>   Strive thy form and soul to save.
> Man of blood, avoid the strand;
>   Demons lurk within the wave."

So saying, the beldame, resuming her burden, struck into a different path. In vain did Albert seek to question her further; she waved her skinny hand, then pointing to her lips and to the sky, intimating that she was forbid to speak more, left him with tottering steps and slow.

Musing on this strange circumstance, he could not help conceiving that it had some connection with the appearance of the figure he had seen on the beach. He also thought of the words of Pierce Gherkin relative to the ocean fiend, and, impelled by curiosity directed his steps to the door of the tailor's cottage, whom he found, as ever, seated cross-legged at his work. On Albert's entrance he arose with all speed to get a stool for his reverence and his holiness, as he styled him, though to him it was an enigma why a man at Albert's time of life, who might marry well and be a rich vassal or even bailiff, should have his head shaved and turn monk.

After a little conversation that it might not seem he had any particular reason for the question, Albert carelessly inquired whence the legend of the Ocean Fiend had sprung, laughingly asking, if he ever made his appearance now? on which the little tailor, devoutly crossing himself, said,—

" Ay, 'tis well for your reverence to talk so, because the fiend has no power over holy men; but I wouldn't for the world say a disrespectful word of him. But a many years ago, when the kingdom was divided among so many kings and princes, one of them, named Red Gorven, was deposed by his people for his cruelty, and driven to this side of the island, where he was hospitably received by Vorkestern, king of Kent; but when, charmed by the beauty of the country, he wished to settle and collect his followers, Vorkestern would give him no land; for, showing him the map of Kent, Vorkestern proved that all its fair land was allotted, and the property of some one, from whom it could not be taken. ' But,' said Vorkestern, ' if you can find any land that I know not of, you shall be welcome to build a city on it, and bring your friends to people it, on condition that you pay tribute to me as your feudal lord, and at your death the city to devolve to me and the heirs to the crown of Kent.' Red Gorven, though he agreed to the conditions, was extremely troubled in his mind. How was it possible that he could find land in Kent that the king and people wotted not of? While one day wandering on the shore, and thinking what he should do for land, he came to the rocks, and while climbing over them, he saw a low cave, the mouth of which was overgrown with sea-weed; star-fish, and curious shells lay strewed on its floor. Upon entering the cave, which was small, an opening led to another, in the centre of which was an altar, and a book filled with curious characters. Half of this cave was dry, and half was deep water, through which, by reflection, the cave was lighted. While standing by the altar, and looking on the water, which seemed more agitated than even the open sea, suddenly it began to boil and bubble like a caldron on a huge fire. Alarmed at this appearance, Red Gorven could not but keep his eyes rivetted on the water, from which presently arose an immense conch shell, made into a chariot, drawn by beautiful white sea-horses, with green manes, fins instead of hoofs, and fishes' tails, instead of their hind quarters. Inside of the chariot was a figure, with scales all over, with finny wings to his back, and fins over his hands and feet. His face was that of a handsome young man, with black hair and beard, and a coral coronet on his brow.

" ' Gorven,' he cried, ' be of good heart; land and city shall be thine, so that thou will yield it up at a certain time, with all its inhabitants.'

" ' I cannot speak for others,' Gorven said, ' but I will be thy slave so thou wilt give me the land required.'

" Well, the Ocean Fiend—for it was he—leaned upon his coral wand, and seemed in a brown study for a few minutes ; then at length he said,—

" Well, Gorven, I consent, taking your own security for the land ; your soul is not worth much, for it's a bad one ; but you shall have the land, and when rent day comes, I must take what I can find.'

" So Gorven agreed to sell his soul for a hundred years more to live, and he signed the book on the altar. The Ocean Fiend then waved his coral wand, and the sea rolled back from where Stonar now stands, so called because the rocks were all ready hewn into stone for building, and were piled up in pyramids. Then Gorven went to Vorkestern and said that he had found land, and entreated that he might have leave to engage workmen and masons to build the city. Vorkestern, surprised that Gorven should have found land in Kent, not known to him or his people, went forth with all his wise men and the heads of the people to see this newly-discovered terra-firma, which, when they saw, they were indeed amazed at.

" The grant was given for him to build the city and hire workmen ; and now all those that had been friendly to him he sent to ; and he invited all artisans and foreigners, and soon peopled his city. And when the hundred years were coming to an end, in order to atone for his wickedness he built the monastery, and conse-crated it to St. Mark, that the saint might plead for him when the Ocean Fiend brought his suit against him. In time he died. He would be taken into the chapel as he was dying, and there buried, directly under the altar-piece, that the fiend might not be able to get at him, body or soul. Lately the fiend has been on the look out again, and I understand he says that he'll be paid his price or he'll have his land again."

Albert could not refrain from a hearty laugh at the ludicrous story the tailor's credulity and invention had given birth to ; but Gherkin was not to be laughed out of his belief. He adhered to his text stoutly,—

" For," said he, " in Red Gorven's coffin is the parchment with the agreement."

" I thought you said that he signed the book on the altar," observed Albert.

" Yes," said the tailor, " that was for the fiend's satisfaction ; but this parch-ment is a copy of the original, for the use of Gorven and his heirs."

Albert smiled at the tailor's ready wit ; and, rising to depart, asked him if he had any more tales as true and excellent as that was. And the tailor, not seeing the sneer, rose, and rummaging a large chest in the corner, drew from it a roll of parch-ment or paper—not to be ascertained which by the colour ; this he put, with great solemnity, into Albert's hand, enjoining him to take great care of it, for that it was inestimable. But few of the laity could read at that time of day, therefore Pierce was justly proud of his book and his learning. Albert, thanking him sarcastically for the valuable loan, which he saw was entitled " Shipton," placed it in his bosom, and left the domicile. Again his brain wandered, and, absorbed in thought, he had walked a considerable distance without noticing it ; at length, looking around, he found himself on the sea beach, about a mile from Stonar.

The sun had sunk below the horizon, and the shades of evening were gathering around, the waves lashed the shore, and the noise of the agitated shingle seemed to mock the foam of the bursting billow. At this moment his eye was caught by an object to the left ; turning to have a full view of it, on a rock, parallel to him, not more than a hundred yards removed, stood the dark figure seen on the night of his return. A black cloak enveloped it ; a hat of the same colour, with a broader brim than usually worn in those days, and green drooping feathers, was the only announcement of his appearance, and he held his drapery close up to his eyes. The features, therefore, were impossible to be discerned, putting aside the uncertain light and the distance. Yet it appeared that he was busily contemplating Albert, who, for some time sat gazing on the stranger, who seemed as immoveable as the rock he stood on. The rapid flight of an osprey, or sea-eagle, attracting the momentary attention of Albert, when again he turned his eyes towards the figure, it was gone.

It could not have reached the shore, for the rocks ran out into the sea, and it must take any man, however agile, five or six minutes at least, to have cleared them. There was no promontory to hide him, yet no vestige could be seen. Startled by the mysterious circumstance, Albert arose and approached the spot, to ascertain if there was any outlet, or place of concealment; but after the most minute search he was convinced that not even a rabbit could be concealed in any cavity there. Disappointed, astonished, and even alarmed, he returned to the convent, and sought his room. On the day following he was to become one of the brotherhood in form. Urban and Antonio had both retired to their cells, and Albert prepared to pass the night in uncomfortable wakefulness; the thoughts of the past and future racking his tortured brain, till he became almost maddened with reflection. He felt assured that some connexion existed between the mysterious figure and the warning of the witch of the wood. To dismiss these thoughts, or at all events divert his mind from dwelling so intently on them, he untied the roll given him by the tailor; he found it was a madrigal, or legend, in verse, and with some difficulty deciphered the characters. It was entitled,—

Shipton; or, the Devil's Bride.

In the days of yore, 'tis said,
  Quite tired of a bachelor's life,
Old Nick took it into his head
  To travel, and marry a wife.

To the famous old county of York,
  His majesty made quick repair,
Because he had heard the folks talk,
  That the prettiest maidens were there.

Soon a virgin he found to his mind,
  Of parentage humble and poor,
Ignorant, handsome, and kind,—
  They call'd her the "Maid of the Moor."

He pass'd for a nobleman grand,
  Which nobody then could gainsay;
He talk'd of his houses and land,—
  What maiden of York would say nay?

The wedding took place in the night,
  It suited such dark doings best;
While the kinsfolk to witness the sight,
  Came from north, from east, and from west.

They all were assembled by seven,—
  Good simple plain holiday folks;
They waited till half-past eleven,
  And then 'gan to think it a hoax.

The church clock had just struck a dozen,
  The bride was with sorrow o'ercast,
When out bawls each uncle and cousin,
  "By goles, he is coming at last!"

Now out they all ran to the door,
  But quick in affright they ran back,
For the bridegroom, and twenty men more,
  Had come to the wedding in black.

Black were their plumes, and black were their clothes,
  And black were the coursers they rode;
They look'd like a flight of ravens or crows—
  It was certes a singular mode.

Every odd man was given a torch,
  And all to the church did repair;
But were met by the priest outside of the porch,
  Who married the young couple there.

Amongst the gay kinsfolk were many old men,
 But the priest had been ne'er seen before;
Nor ever was seen by any, till then,
 A marriage take place at the door.

Cold was the bridegroom, and chill his embrace,
 As the woman was heard to declare,
But such a wedding most sure did take place,
 And a daughter was born to the pair.

See p. 76.

Ere twelve months were over, he found he'd a shrew,
 Which too oft is the case in a wife;
Till one day, in a passion, the devil he flew
 Away from the devil's own life.

The daughter, in time, a name did require,
 But the father's had never been known;
So the mother, not knowing the name of the sire
 Was obliged for to give her her own.

The daughter was ugly, yet she was rich,
 In gifts both prophetic and strange;
A teller of fortunes—known for a witch,
 Who her form in a minute could change.

Mother Shipton, yclept, and the peasants declare
Faggots had been her just doom,
For oft in a storm, they've seen, in the air,
Her riding across a birchbroom.

Her prophecies living, prove this to be true,
Her parentage certain and plain;
So young men and maidens, all mind what you do;
Lest the devil should come here again.

In a rage Albert threw the parchment down, vexed that he should have been so weak as to peruse it. It was idle rhyme, and another had not been thus moved, but it seemed as though a demon's influence was exerted to cast a spell around him. And while he strove to shake the fearful feeling off, everything around seemed to favour the superstitious belief, and fill his soul with dread. In the dead hour of midnight he heard a slight knock at his door—opening it, Urban entered.

"Well, Albert," he cried, "or as you will soon be Father Ernest, as I, John Beauchamp, am now Urban. How stands your stomach for the ceremony? pity to lose those luxuriant curls, and shroud that manly form in a guise more becoming old women, than gallant spirits born for martial deeds. Wilt thou be mad enough to resign the world for a life of mumbling paternosters—wilt thou, bully boy?"

Much as he was accustomed to Urban's free style, still the profane language and the holy vestments seemed so incongruous, that he gazed at him with surprise.

"What dost stare so for? I love thee, and if thou hast the heart to knock this holy abbot on the head, and half a score of his lazy satellites, here is a hand shall join thee—I shrink not."

"Peace, Urban; you speak loud, and forget who may be listening. What you talk of, could I persuade myself to act so vile a part, would require more aid than thine."

"More aid may be got," said Urban, "and beyond weak mortal powers, an you have a mind to prove thyself worthy of the form thou hast received, there are spirits ——"

Laying his hand on Albert's, and then observing the word had shaken him, said—

"Gallant spirits, that are thy friends."

"Wouldst thou have me doom my own soul to endless torment?" said Albert.

"A child's tale—mockery all," said Urban, his eyes sparkling with unearthly fire.

"Do you then doubt the vengeance of an angry Creator, or do you doubt that being's existence? You must, to argue thus."

"What is His existence to thee, if He treats thee ill? retaliation is the law of nature; if He forgets thee, are you not justified in forgetting Him; then are powers kinder to their votaries, that uphold them through every peril."

Base as Albert had become, blasphemy, and a doubt of the Divine Being, had never crossed his thought. He had offended, he knew, and he shrank from the idea of divine vengeance. To have braved, or mocked the Deity, had not entered his thought, for his soul's price.

"In the name of the great Being you are now offending, cease, I command you," said Albert.

Urban arose instantly, with a most demoniac expression on his face, and leaving the cell, said, as he held the door,—

"Virtuous robber, holy murderer, pious miscreant—when you tax Urban next with being profane, forget not to inflict a penance on thyself for hypocrisy. Where is Rachel? where Isabel? where the wretched family burnt at the Brian Farm? Ha! ha! ha!"

So saying, he slammed to the door, while a laugh struck upon the ear of Albert, that froze his blood. He had, indeed, deserved reproaches, and felt that now a cloistered life alone would soothe his soul; but if such as Urban, like the screech-owl, alarmed the frighted soul, what hope was there? At the moment the cell door opened, and the holy father abbot entered. Confused and surprised, Albert arose, and welcomed his superior, who seating himself, gazed for a minute in Albert's face, and then said,—

" By our holy order, I could almost fancy what I dreamt had indeed been sooth, your countenance speaks horror and despair."

" Your dream, holy sir," said Albert.

" Ay, marry," said Jocelyn, " I dreamt that thy life, both here and hereafter, had been in jeopardy. Methought I saw a fiend at thy couch side, you writhing beneath his demon grasp. ' Pray for thy soul,' I cried, ' thy mortal part is doomed.' I heard thy screams, and rushea towards thee – suddenly a sea of blood seemed to rise between us, and I was lost in the crimson wave. When I awoke, still, to my thinking, I heard thy screams, and hurried hither, in the belief that something terrific had affected thy temporal welfare ; and your blanched brow would seem to corroborate the fact. What have we here?" stooping and picking up Pierce Gherkin's " Shipton."

Albert felt his face glow, and he could have sunk through the earth. The brow of Jocelyn knitted as he perused the rhyming legend, at the end of which he placed it in the lamp, nor took his eyes from it, till it was reduced to ashes.

" Well might I dream," cried Jocelyn, " of thy soul's danger ; and you devote the hours that should be employed in prayer and penitence, to wicked idle tales as these. By my order I could find in my heart to double thy probation, but for thy soul's sake. When thou art summoned to the altar, I charge thee, abjure the world, save thyself ere it be too late."

Sternly bidding him prepare for the solemnity, the abbot left him, pacing his cell in a state of mind bordering on distraction, overwrought and perplexed in the extreme. The matin bell now summoned the holy brotherhood to the church. While there, Urban came, as was his wont, beside him, and the prayers over, inquired kindly after his spirits. Shocked at his duplicity, Albert upbraided him, and cautioned him either to avoid him, or such themes as he chose to expatiate on last night. To his utmost astonishment, Urban averred that he had never left his own cell, nor knew what he meant. On Albert, repeating the accusation, Urban protested his innocence by an oath so solemn, that Albert feeling a horrible conviction flash on his mind, became insensible, and was only brought to by the utmost attention of the fathers, who imputed it to a dread or dislike to the approaching ceremony ; but on his recovery, he seemed most anxious it should take place, being convinced that he had been tampered with by some wicked power, and he hoped, when taken to the bosom of the church, to enjoy calm thoughts and holy peace.

His hair having been cut off in the sacristy, and the habit of the monastery put on him, he was led by two monks to the altar, and kneeling before the abbot, formally abjured the world, devoting himself to the service of the church. On such occasions the church is always open to strangers, yet but few were there. Behind a pillar, a female form might be seen anxiously watching the young brother's looks ; and when Albert would steal a look towards that quarter, she shrank still further from sight, till the ceremony completed, and the jubilate was chanted by the brotherhood, in full deep chorus. As the abbot blessed him, she sank upon her knees, and remained in prayer some time. Nor was she an only interested spectator. As Albert knelt to receive the holy blessing, his eye wandered mechanically to the door, and the figure he had seen on the beach the last night, passed by the portal, and stood at the great window, looking into the church, his remarkable figure challenging the attention of all, which, when he saw, he vanished in as sudden a manner as before, on the rock. A chill came over Albert's heart, and but for his ghostly supporters, must have fallen.

The ceremony over, he was again led to his cell. Passing the gallery, he looked up at Sabina, who waved her handkerchief. He was pleased to see she smiled upon him – it was a seraph's smile, welcoming a brother angel to the realms of truth. Never did Heloise love Abelard with a purer flame, but he shared not the heart of Abelard, nor was worthy of her. On his return to his cell, he found Cyril waiting for him. He had also witnessed the ceremony, and on Albert's entrance, threw himself in his arms and wept freely. The affectionate boy thought he saw, in Albert's retirement from the world, a loss of Albert's self. The spring would return again, and the violet bloom fresh again, but the world that he had left would smile on him no more—it was a living death.   In vain did Albert pacify him that he could always see him.   Cyril had seen Sabina weep, had caught the infection. He had a note from her, which was eagerly seized by Albert—its words were few.

"Dear Friend,
"Lost to me, you are now restored to yourself.   I now can look upon you as a brother, and shall joy in our correspondence, but we meet no more.   Above all, avoid my father.   But, believe me, thine till death.   "SABINA."

Yes, she loved him—every word and action proved it—and he had put their union now for ever beyond hope.   In secret, he cursed Jocelyn and the baron; wrote a tender epistle to her; this, like a former one, fell into the baron's hands, who, suspecting such a thing, had Cyril seized and searched; the event justified his apprehension, Cyril was committed to the warder's strong room, with orders not to be suffered to leave the castle; Sabina was also confined to her chamber, with the mortification of not knowing whether it was her note or his that was taken, not being allowed to see Cyril.   Of all this Albert was ignorant, and was surprised that he saw not Cyril.

Some few days after, a strange idea having seized him that his end was fast approaching, he resolved to see the witch of the wood, and learn whether he or Sabina should die first, or whether it was worth while to hold a life that must continue without hope.   Having formed his resolution, he sought the sibyl's cottage; she was seated at the door, basking in the sun; he had saluted the hag, and placed a golden token in her hand, when, ere he could state his request, she said,—

"Away! there is blood upon thy hand; leave me this instant, and speed to thy convent, or you will commit a murder in the hour."

Astonished and startled, he proposed his question; again she warned him hence, but he refused to go till she should answer his questions, at which she angrily arose and making a circle round her with an ebon wand she wrote down his name and Sabina's, then threw some grains of wheat, she then muttered some words in a deep guttural tone and then paused, a raven immediately come out of the passage and eat up the grains that had fallen on Sabina's name, but left those on his; after this she stamped with her foot several times, then seemed disappointed, and removing a green cloth that hung before a mirror formed of polished steel—that being the material of which they were made previous to the use and improvement of glass—after looking into this she resumed her seat.   Albert urged her to tell him the conclusion she had come to.

Sabina, she said, would die first, but he would not be long after, but so dark a cloud hung over his destiny after her death that it was impossible to get to know all, and what she did know she would not tell.   He offered her a purse, she declined it; he then wished to look into the mirror himself, which having done, he saw a tower standing up in the water, and a figure, as of himself, at the top; in the water, and as rising from it, a female figure pale and shrouded—it was Sabina.   The waters now got troubled, and the mist increasing on the mirror he could see no more; after a few minutes it subsided, and a flat, green, level spot presented itself, with Richborough Castle on the cliff; he asked the sibyl what it meant, she shook her head but returned no answer, waved her hand to him to leave, and went into her cottage.   Albert returning into the wood vexed and dissatisfied, he was the dupe of juggling fiends and could believe nothing.   Suddenly he found he had taken the wrong turning, and was then standing on the very spot where the baron surprised him and Sabina.   When he thought of the events that had occurred since he last stood there, his indignation rose against the baron and Arnold; the latter was no more, the former even now seemed to be the arbiter of his fate, and exert a cruel influence over him.   Jocelyn, the abbot, had told him that it required the utmost stretch of his ability and interest to save him, the baron was so inveterate, which proceeded from Sabina's constant refusal to accept the hand of any that he offered to her.   She was an only child, and the title and estates would pass to another branch of the family, if Sabina never married.

His sole hope was, that when Albert had become a monk, and she was convinced of it, she would in time change, and yet obey his wish. With this idea alone, he permitted Jocelyn to receive him into the monastery of St. Mark, as she would herself be convinced of his being now lost to her for ever, but it in nothing abated his hatred to him, for having dared to look up to a Norman baron's daughter.

At this moment a portly figure crossed his path. Albert started. The person paused, too ; it was the baron. As if he had seen a serpent, did the Norman stand and gaze upon the monk. He knew him, the hated lineaments were still the same. Suspecting that he had come to effect an interview with Sabina, his rage increased.

" Wretch !" he exclaimed. " Why had I not slain thee on this spot eight years since ? Liar and slave, thou comest to entice my daughter from her duty."

" You are wrong, my lord. My presence here was as little expected by myself as your lordship. I had no intention of seeing the Lady Sabina, and your lordship will do well to consider that I am now a servant of the Catholic and apostolic see of Rome, not of any temporal master, and any insult to me will be revenged by the church. You know its power, my lord." The baron foamed with rage.

" Villain !" he cried, " thou art my slave—a born serf on my estate. Another word, and I'll cleave thee to the chine. Liar ! is it well, the servant of Rome to disgrace the habit of his order, by a falsity base as himself? look on this billet, and dissemble longer if you can."

Albert saw with mortification his lost billet. Had Cyril turned traitor, or had Sabina betrayed him to her father? He demanded of the baron of whom he had obtained it ?

" From the youth, that, snake-like, has turned to sting the hand that fed him ; but he dies ere the morning."

" Not for you soul, lord baron," cried Albert. " Harm that boy—if that a hair of his head be injured, you shall deeply and bitterly repent it."

" Do you dare to threaten ?" said Fitzormond. " 'Tis well. You shall receive his corse ere daylight."

" At your peril," rejoined the monk.

Mad with rage, and being threatened, which the Norman spirit never could brook, he drew his dagger, and seized on Albert. They struggled in mortal enmity. The foot of the monk slipped, and he fell, dragging his powerful antagonist down with him. The hands of both were on each other's throats. Albert called to the baron to release him, for his soul's sake.

" Never !" cried Fitzormond, " they life, or mine ;" and being now the uppermost, he placed his knee on Albert's breast, while he sought to plunge the dagger into his throat. " Life is sweet—revenge is sweeter."

Albert used his utmost strength, but trifling, when compared to the baron's, but, by one lucky violent effort, he wrenched the dagger from his sinewy grasp, and the next instant it had pierced his heart. The baron fell on him with a groan, and expired, drenching his adversary in his blood. By struggling, he contrived to get himself from under the body, and gazing on what he had done, though in self-defence, horror possessed his heart, and terror adding strength and swiftness, he fled. Rushing through the wood, avoiding the approaches to the town, and making his way to the beach with the intention of throwing himself into the ocean, and so close a wretched existence. On reaching the shore, he sank down unable to move, and had the tide been on the return, his wish would have been fulfilled, while yet he lay insensible. When he came to himself, in consequence of the sea breeze, the remembrance of what he had done rushed upon his brain. His monk's gown was torn and saturated with blood, his hands and throat wounded in many places, by the baron's dagger, which lay by his side—his brow burnt, and his very brain ached with intensity of horror. He cast his eyes wildly around, nor knew till then, that he was not alone. The figure in the cloak stood by his side—his form was noble and commanding, his face was pale, and his hair and beard of raven jet; his eyebrows high, and arched, and his eyes gleamed with the tiger's horrid glare. Rising as swiftly as his bruised limbs would permit him, Albert exclaimed,—

" Being of terror, who and what are you?"

" Your friend," exclaimed the figure, " and a true friend ; if you deserve my friendship, learn to take council. Had you obeyed the old woman, you would have saved yourself from this last crime."

" You know me, then?" exclaimed the horror-struck Albert.

" Better than you know yourself," was the reply. " Fear not—wealth and power may yet be yours—Sabina, too."

" How !" Albert exclaimed. " Say but that, prove but that, and I will be your slave."

" 'Tis well," cried the unknown ; " some one comes ; fear not, they are your friends. At the dead of night seek the church vaults, and there will I meet you."

" I swear it !" cried Albert.

" Enough," cried the other. " Keep to your promise—tremble to break it. Palter with me, and beware of the Ocean Fiend !"

At the dread name Albert sank again insensible, and the demon vanished.

The persons came up, and proved to be his friends Urban and Antonio. Chafing his temples, they quickly recovered him. Antonio, who had often heard him breathe vengeance on Fitzormond, guessed the real truth immediately. The business now was to get Albert into the monastery, and manage so that it should appear he had not quitted it that day. Urban, who had several gowns, brought one from the convent, and Albert being attired in it, his own was buried beneath a tree near the beach ; he was then removed to the convent, and, by a back door, conveyed to his cell by the two friends. The marks on his throat died away in a short time, and the cuts on his hands and neck were not much more than scratches, that could not be very observable.

After instructing him as to the course he should pursue—for terror had so far unnerved him that he was as a very child, and the friends almost feared his betraying himself. However, fixing him in prayer, they left him in the cell. In a short time after, a noise and confusion was heard. Albert's heart trembled in his bosom ; a crowd was heard outside his cell, and in another moment the abbot, Urban, and Antonio, with others, entered the cell, the rest waiting without. Chill ran the blood in the murderer's veins.

" Albert," said Jocelyn, " I come to announce a most dreadful event ——"

" The Baron Fitzormond has been murdered," said Urban.

For which he was severely reprimanded by Joscelyn ; but the wily Urban saw the state of Albert's mind and countenance, and said this that the knowledge of the dreadful event might excuse the look of horror so plain to be seen on Albert's face. Besides which, he feared questions being asked, in answering which, Albert might have inadvertently betrayed a knowledge of the murder before he had been told of it. On hearing of the dreadful event, Albert staggered, and the increasing paleness of his countenance and real emotion spoke not much in his favour.

" You will not be surprised, Albert," said the abbot, " that in consequence of the known bad blood between you and the baron, and his body not having been rifled—thus p'ainly proving that he was not waylaid by robbers—I say, you will not be surprised when I tell you that you are the suspected murderer."

" The eternal heavens !" cried Albert.

" I'll swear he never left the convent yesterday," exclaimed Urban, Antonio, and a few others, some of whom they had suborned, and some who really did believe they had seen him.

" I am most happy," cried the abbot, " to hear this ; yet all will have to be proved. One thing will surely point the murder out."

Albert's soul seemed to die away within him. What proof could they bring forward ? Jocelyn resumed this subject :—

" A strip of cloth was found near the spot, evidently belonging to a monk's gown, it comes from the front part. Ernest, you must let your gown be examined, let the officers enter."

Two officers entering the cell, the gown of Albert was narrowly examined—the result may be supposed. The abbot embraced him, saying,—

"My soul is satisfied, but public justice must be so likewise. But I will not yield to the secular arm—you shall be tried. He that was slain was my father's brother's son, but one remove from my very flesh, and by blood most certainly the same; I am, therefore, bound to avenge his death, but I will not suffer the privileges of my order to be violated. You shall be tried—justice, nature demand it; but you shall be tried by the spiritual, not temporal power. You will repair to the monastery of St. Augustin, at Canter ury; the pope's legate is now there, investigating the horrible murder of Thomas a Becket, the Archbishop."

Accordingly, all was prepared for the solemn ceremony of giving up a brother of St. Mark's Monastery to the care of the Augustin monks of Canterbury on the morrow; during which, he was not made a prisoner in his cell or any restraint put upon him, further than not being allowed to quit the walls, or pass the gates, where the porters kept strict watch; and the temporal power were posted outside, not fifty yards from each other, and keeping unwearied vigil through the night; each party seemed convinced as to the innocence or guilt of the accused, as the sentiments of the parties preponderated.

The town of Stonar was equally divided. By some Albert was extolled, and by some, who could not pierce through the mystery that ever seemed to envelope him, condemned instanter.

He had a long conference with Urban, when the friends planned the death of the witch; since, if she revealed their meeting, the fate of Albert was decided.

He had never revealed to either Urban or Antonio the secret of his conference with the fiend—that secret was kept inviolate in his own bosom. In the dead of the night Urban slumbered in his seat, and Antonio had already retired to his cell. The hour of his departure drew near; leaving Urban to enjoy his dreams, he arose, and, taking the lamp, which cast a blue and pale light, he went to the sacristy, where the keys were usually kept. The monastery was no prison, and the keys were suspended on nails with numbers affixed. The sacristan slept, but the key of the vault was in its place. Taking the sexton's lamp, in preference to his own, that seemed weak in supply, he descended to the underground department of the chapel. As soon as he got to the vault door, he searched for his glass dagger, which he ever kept with him concealed, though, in the wild confusion of the baron's struggle, he was unable to clutch it. Against a supernatural being it was useless; but he sometimes suspected mortal treachery.

Turning the key in the rusty ward, he threw open the door of the vault. The foul mephitic vapour nearly overcame him. Suffering it for a few minutes to be rarified by the purer atmosphere, he entered, lifting the torch high to cast its light more generally around, for, from the cause above mentioned, it burned dim, and a misty halo seemed to gather around it.

Proceeding further, he rested the torch in a niche or arm made for the purpose, and proceeded to take a survey of the place; it wanted yet a quarter of the time appointed by the fiend. Several gigantic effigies in armour lay on tombs this having been the nave formerly, but sunk in an earthquake, and the monuments intended to meet men's eyes and tell the tale—a lesson on the mutability of all human affairs, and how vain the attempt of man to perpetuate a name.

Immediately under the altar was a plain black marble sarcophagus, on which was inscribed, "Ranulph Gorven, Founder—Requiescat in pace." It was extremely old and dilapidated. The lid had been broken by some accident, and the coffin was visible, also of stone. With a little labour he removed the top of the sarcophagus, and soon found that the lid of the coffin was moveable, having been constructed with hinges and a sort of spring, rendered useless by time and bad usage. A few bones, part of the skull, the vertebræ, and the thigh-bones yet remained; the rest was gone to dust. Some drapery, yellow with age, a rude dagger, and the scabbard of a sword, were in the coffin, but nothing else was to be seen; so that the marvellous tale of Pierce Gherkin seemed without foundation.

As he passed his hand off the drapery, he observed a signet ring on the bony hand, rudely made, with a ruby in its centre. As Albert was trying to remove it on to his own finger, he perceived, a roll of parchment curiously folded, and tied around with gold cord. This he quickly abstracted, and, taking it to the torch, endeavoured to make out the writing ; but with the damp and age a great part was illegible. It appeared to have been signed with blood ; the characters were now a faint yellow ; the name of Ranulph Gorven was perceptible, and that of Vorkestern was also to be seen. The subject of the writing was not to be ascertained, but its antiquity made it valuable ; but Albert would have given his right hand to have read it.

Raising his eyes from it, he started with surprise ; for, standing on the sarcophagus, appeared the Ocean Fiend, his scales glittering faintly in the red gleam of the torch. The fins over his hands resembled gauntlets ; his coronet of high sharp points, resembled the head-dress of that imaginary being ; yet there was something terrible in his look, and grand in his carriage ; he had a small sceptre in his hand, formed of a branch of white coral.

"Hold !" he cried ; "is it not enough to destroy the living—wherefore plunder the dead ?"

Albert held the parchment in his hand,—

"Does Gorven sleep in peace ?" he cried. "Burn the document."

Albert held it to the torch. The fiend had stepped from the sarcophagus and seemed to await the result with interest. The parchment, on being set fire to, emitted sparks, and gave notice as though it would explode. Albert, therefore, threw it down in the front of the sarcophagus ; it caused a great smoke as it burned, and as it cleared away, on the sarcophagus, and with one foot on the coffin lid stood a stalwart form of a man, with a white and venerable looking beard, the mustaches forming part of it, and of equal length, and the hair of his head falling gracefully on his shoulders. His dress resembled that of the ancient patriarchs, a crimson drapery enveloping the greater part of his figure ; a buskined boot, formed of untanned leather, covered the leg, nearly resembling the Greek hose ; the toes were bare, and the soles of his boot were made of wood ; a plain gold circlet, without fashion or ornament, or without a cap, bound his temples, in the style of our ancient British kings or princes of the heptarchy. His hand was extended to Gilbert as though he demanded restitution of the parchment. Observing it burning, the figure was about to step down to secure the remains, when his eye caught the figure of the fiend ; his form seemed to shake horribly ; his countenance, hitherto so mild and placid, was dreadfully convulsed with emotion. With his two hands he seemed to repel the fiend, and, shrinking with horror, he appeared to sink by degrees into the sarcophagus ; a thick smoke again rose from the parchment, and the figure was lost to human eye.

From out of his sceptre the Ocean Fiend now produced a scroll, in which Wealth, Honour, and Sabina were named.

"Behold," said the fiend, "this I promise, with safety in thy present strait ; yet must you be wary. When you fail in attaining an object, blame not me, but your own want of resolution, which has brought every evil on you."

"Even fiends, then, deal in truth," thought Albert.

"The manner by which you are to obtain what I have promised will occur to you as the opportunity presents itself ; by this bond you dispose of yourself and monastery, and yield all up when I require."

"At what time—how long am I to exist ?" asked Albert.

"That depends upon the fates, and not on me ; enough that you live to enjoy the blessings I have promised."

A pen and inkstand were now produced, and Albert signed. The fiend then seized the paper ; with a horrid discordant laugh he leaped upon the sarcophagus, his marine wings extending ; then with a voice resembling musical recitative, he said or sang, the following,—

> "From coral rocks I come,
>   From ocean's stormy bed,
> O'er earth's gay face to roam,
>   By mischief led,
> The sons of earth to ensnare,
>   Who are from virtue wean'd ;
> Why, then, silly fools beware
>   Of the Ocean Fiend !"

See page 77.

A clap of thunder shook the place, and Albert falling to the ground, suddenly found himself in his own cell, with Urban just catching him from falling off the couch.

"My dear friend," cried Urban, "you must not give way thus to your feelings. You have prated terribly in your dreams, and just now seized the pen in the ink-stand by you, and wrote your name upon the couch. See, the signature is yet damp, and in another instant you would have fallen."

"Great Heaven!" said Albert, "did I not descend into the vault after taking the key from the sacristan's room? Did I not enter the vault beneath the altar? Did I not see the sacrophagus and shade of Gorven? Did I not see the dreaded form, too, of ——"

"Holy St. Dominic! I feared this," said Urban. "Your wits are disturbed—your brain turning. In the first place, you have never moved out of this room; in the next, you could not get the key of the vaults under the church from the sacristan, as there are no vaults there, the vaults being in the cemetery, which is behind the chapel. Gorven, the founder, has no sacrophagus that any one knows of, nor where he is buried. It is said beneath the altar, but I doubt the fact; the chapel and altar are recent erections; not a hundred years built. Gorven founded this city before the time of Edward the Confessor; and of whom do you speak and seem so much to dread?"

Albert was confounded; eagerly he asked if the affair of the baron were also imaginary, but was too painfully undeceived. At that moment a lay brother announced that the escort was ready to convey Albert to Canterbury. Urban promised to see the old woman, and if necessary to take measures to prevent her prating; as it was, she did not see the deed committed, and her prophetic talent would not avail in a common court of justice, much less an ecclesiastical court,

On taking leave of Albert, Jocelyn said,—

"Though compelled to stand in the opposite characters of denouncer and superior witness in your favour, you shall have justice done you. The legate is a severe man, and the affair of the Archbishop A'Becket will make him doubly strict as to a murderer. I tell you this not to intimidate you, but to prevent intimidation; irresolution has been your ruin!" Albert started—it was the language of the fiend. It had indeed been Albert's besetting sin. "You will also remember that there is one point in this which operates in your favour; the privileges and rights of the church have been violated by the entrance of the knights to the cathedral, which should have been a sanctuary, even to a robber. The legate was about to punish this severely, and now an instance occurs of the civil power seizing on a monk, and trying him for the murder of a Norman. Be assured, if he discovers that you are wrongfully accused, he will punish your oppressors. Farewell! In the court we know not each other. Benedicte."

Before leaving the room, Albert ventured to name Sabina and Cyril; the former he was told would appear as his accuser: all his firmness fled, and he was compelled to lean against the wall to support himself. Cyril was to be produced, but in what position Jocelyn could not inform him. Albert, before leaving, told him the name of Cyril's father, and that he was a relative of the Fitzormond family, a circumstance which had escaped him till the baron threatened his death. He had learned it by hearing the abbot mention the name as akin to them, and it is to be remembered that there was but little time when Cyril accompanied them from the cavern of the robbers to explain matters, and there he had been called by his christian name only. The circumstance was hardly worth noticing, but that Albert, in his mentioning it to the abbot, inconsiderately, said,—

"I told the baron so when he threatened to take his life for taking the letter."

"When?" said Jocelyn.

Albert recollected himself, and said,—

"Some time since."

This, as it will appear afterwards, had weight on his trial. Jocelyn looked grave, and ordered the lay brother to tell the officers they were ready. They had a vehicle at the gate, something similar to a small hearse, but higher, used for the purpose of carrying prisoners. Its four wheels were broad, and clumsy, and the two oxen that drew it tugged hard to get it along. The deep ruts and the jolts that Albert received every now and then were enough to dislocate every bone in his body, there being no springs invented then.

After a weary journey they arrived at the gates of Canterbury at eight o'clock in the evening, though they had started at four o'clock in the morning. The distance at that time of day was about three-and-twenty miles, and they had been sixteen hours performing it, in consequence of the heavy, bad roads, and the slow pace of the oxen.

On his arrival he was lodged in the convent of the Augustin monks, whose pride and insolence at that time exceeded all that could be conceived, they having the honour of lashing the weak King Henry on his naked shoulders, for the share he had in the murder of Thomas A'Becket, a degradation and insult that was remembered, and bitterly revenged by his grandson, Henry III., who made it a pretext for removing their convent, and taking away all their privileges.

Albert was conducted to a cell, and supplied only with bread and water. At night an Augustin monk came to question him as to the crime imputed, but Albert kept most stubbornly silent. They had not entertained him sufficiently well to make any disclosures to them, even had he been so disposed.

The pope's legate being informed of the nature of Albert's case, gave notice that it should be brought forward immediately, that the rights of the church might be fully proved, and the crime of murder punished. Indeed a more welcome event could not have happened. Had the murdered man been a churchman it would have suited his holiness better.

In the morning Albert was conducted to the archbishop's palace, where the grand case was being tried, the grand court being fitted up as a court of inquiry, with seats for the dignitaries, the witnesses, and places for the public, as well as for the accused and accuser.

He was first taken into a private chamber, where he was spoken to by the Bishop of Winchester, the Earl of Suffolk, and other great persons, who wished him success, and enjoined him to be firm, for that the late Fitzormond was a nobleman of great power, a special favourite of the king, and, consequently, his kin would have much influence, and would not leave any means untried to discover the murderer, and punish him.

All being in readiness, he was conducted into the great hall to the prisoner's bar. The place was crowded ; the pope's legate was seated on a throne, elevated above all the rest. Next to him, but a little lower, were two chairs, for the Archbishop of Canterbury and the Bishop of Winchester; the former seat being vacant, the chair was filled by a temporal peer, the Earl of Suffolk, the king's almoner. Below them sat six bishops and six judges. At a large table before these sat the clerks and some lawyers, to satisfy the legate on any point of law in an ecclesiastical court. In a case like this there was no pleading by counsel. In a box, with several noblemen, her uncle, and the abbot, sat Sabina, seemingly in great distress of mind, her face concealed by her handkerchief. In a box, on the other side, sat the witnesses for the prosecution. Cyril sat almost by himself. Albert looked round, but did not see the witch of the wood. On a bench, covered with red baize, sat the witnesses for the prisoner, Urban and Antoine, and several other monks; also the tailor, Gherkin, whom, when Albert saw, he could have wished hence, as it was not unlikely that by his chattering he might do more mischief than good. In a part of the hall, by himself, leaning against a pillar, was the awful figure, and in his hand was a roll of parchment, certainly the very same that Albert had signed. He would have given the world to have got to him.

The public accuser than arose, and stated that the Lord Baron Fitzormond, Castellan of Richborough, and holder of the Isle of Thanet, by right of lineal descent from Godfrey Fitzormond, stirrup holder to William the Conqueror, had been found on such a day murdered in a small wood, or plantation, adjacent to Richborough Castle. The blow had been taken with singular good intent, the weapon having pierced the centre of the heart. He had not been robbed, but it appeared, from the appearance of the deceased baron's apparel, that he had been struggling violently with the villain or villains who had attacked him. That a minute inquiry had been entered into, and suspicion could only fall on Father Ernest, a monk of St. Mark, but known formerly and better as Albert Durand. The most deadly hatred existed between them ; each had been heard to threaten the other, and the friends of either party had even prevented them from meeting, in the assured conviction that bloodshed would be the result. On the day before the murder Albert had abjured the world, and become a monk, induced to it by Jocelyn, abbot of St. Mark, cousin to the baron, who had an interest in urging it, that he might be convinced that the Lady Sabina would be safe from his importunities. These things premised, and the confusion exhibited by the monk at being acquainted with it, gave grounds for this examination.

All men knowing pro or con in this affair, are commanded in the name of the Most High, and by order of pope and cardinals, backed by the warrant of our good King Henry Second, to speak and disclose all that they know, favour and affection set aside. Blessed be the man who obeys these commands, and cursed the stock of them that oppose and thwart the ends of justice."

This exordium being finished, the legate said,—

" Prisoner, you have heard the accusation. Do you plead guilty, or not guilty?"

" Not guilty, by my holy order," answered Albert.

All the witnesses were now sworn, and all else concerned. The legate then arose from his seat, and said,—

" My lords spiritual and temporal. While I regret the fate of the noble Norman, I rejoice that here an example can be shown that the Catholic church, while it protects its members, and severely punishes its enemies, will ever do justice to all. A layman is murdered, and a churchman is accused ; but lately a churchman was murdered, and the layman proved to have committed the most barbarous murder on record, and Rome demands justice. She wills it, nor shall royalty dare to screen the culprits. Here, if the churchman be guilty, we will be equally as strict in rendering justice, as exacting it. Who, on the part of the deceased, proceeds to the accusation ?"

The clerk stated, the Lady Sabina, daughter to the deceased baron, and Jocelyn, termed her uncle, but in reality, cousin to the baron; the disparity of years between the cousins, causing the error inserted in the writ.

" Jocelyn rising, bowed to the legate, and said,—

" Your holiness will pardon the emotion of my young relative, who, I am sorry to observe, was once fondly attached to the prisoner, who was every way unworthy of her. Judge then, what her feelings must be, thus compelled to declare her conviction that the monk is the murderer."

" Is that her conviction?" asked the legate. " If speech be too painful, lift up thy hand, young lady in approval. Is it your conviction that your father fell by his hand?"

The whole court was silent. Albert looked towards her. She turned her head from him, she seemed to endure a dreadful struggle with her feelings, and then raising her hand, she sank back into the seat. It was now the opinion of nearly the whole court, that he must be guilty, as she would never have accused him without good grounds. Albert seemed violently affected by her decision.

Jocelyn then stated, that his first impression was, that Albert had committed the murder, but on going to his cell, it was proved he had not left the convent that day. At this stage of the proceedings, Urban and Antoine both swore to having been with him all day ; and several others, to having seen him several times on the day in question, and at every duty of prayer. The porter of the monastery, a very old man, alone gave evidence to the contrary, He thought he had let him out, but he would not swear to it. Again Jocelyn observed—a piece of a man's gown was found near the baron's body, and the gown of Albert was whole. He had but just been admitted, and had no other garment of that description. This was proved by the storekeeper of the convent, and by the officers who searched his things—no remains of any other gown being found.

That all as yet was in favour of the monk, observed the legate ; he was not bound, nor would any court listen to supposition merely. What was there to criminate the monk?

Though it was against his wish to mention it, said Jocelyn, yet he was bound to avenge a murdered relative. Albert had professed he told the baron of a certain circumstance, or was going to do so, when the baron was threatening him. " Now, to my certain knowledge," said he, " they had never seen each other for eight years, unless they met on the day of the murder. Yet did he state that he had spoken to the baron, and the baron to him. Let this be explained."

Albert cursed his stupidity, and Urban and Antoine each looked daggers at him.

The legate observed that more weight was to be attached to it than it looked, in the first instance, worth. If he had seen the baron, he had surely murdered him.

He called on Albert to explain. Albert felt his invention sharpened, and then stated that Jocelyn had mistaken him, or he had not expressed himself sufficiently plain, by saying that he had told the baron his meaning by note or letter. He had written to him, though he had not dared to address him.

"Who was the bearer?"

Albert pointed to Cyril.

"Have you ever taken letters from the prisoner to Richborough Castle?" asked the legate.

This question was put exactly as Cyril would have wished it, since now he could conscientiously say, "yes."

"Did you ever take letters from the castle to him?"

"Yes."

"From the baron, or his daughter?"

The question was important. Albert looked anxiously at Cyril, who understood it. He answered,—

"When asked to take letters from the castle to the convent, I asked not who wrote them. Sometimes the baron sent notes to the abbot; sometimes the Lady Sabina did. I asked not who wrote them."

The court deemed the answer sufficient, and the abbot's question, which explained nothing, did not impeach the character of Albert, or Father Ernest. The abbot here said, that Cyril was a member of the Fitzormond family, and he thought he should be able to prove, that he was, after himself, next of kin, in the event of the Lady Sabina dying without heirs. Had the baron known it, he would not have been in the degree of a messenger. He had been reared by Albert, who revenged his father's death. He mentioned this, to prove that he, in gratitude to Ernest, might be induced to favour him in his deposition. He was bound to revenge his own family. Cyril answered, that he knew the nature of an oath, that he had nothing to expect from Father Ernest, everything to depend on the Fitzormonds for. He had answered the questions correctly; he had spoken the truth.

Several voices called out for acquittal now, a custom much in use in former times, when the culprit was, according to the opinion of the people, cleared, but they were sternly commanded to be silent.

Just at this moment Pierce Gherkin came forward, and begging pardon of the legate, said he had something which he believed would prove, beyond a doubt, that Albert Durand was as innocent as the sucking pig unborn.

The legate, smiling at the simple manner of the speaker, said he believed it also, and that he was just going to acquit him with honour; "but I will hear you," he added; "as it will confirm all, though it is taking up time, and ere this I had relieved his anxiety; but be as brief as you can."

"I will, your admirable holiness. Heaven love all that's about you. I was looking out of my window—my back window, your blessed comfortableness—when, about a mile off, or that way on, I saw some men very busy, digging a hole in the beach. I've very good eyes, your holiness, and can see into a mile-stone as far as them that pick it, as the saying is. Well, after I had looked at these men a bit longer, says I to myself, your holiness, 'I'll be whipped to death with the bottoms of brown thread, if them men ain't burying some spirits, or wine, or ship plunder, and I may come in for a snacks; so I watches till they went away, and I kept my eye upon the place, which was—let me see—no; not quite a mile—about three quarters distant. I ran all the way; it was just opposite the Piper's Rock. When I gets there, I found the place, your holy excellence, by the earth being freshly turned up. I had taken a spade on my shoulder, all the way; and when I had dug a deuce of a way—excuse that horrible oath, your tremendous holiness—I found these."

With these words, he produced a bundle, which, on being unrolled, appeared to be a monk's cloak, stained with blood, and torn in front. The emotion of Albert and Urban was difficult to conceal; had Albert not held fast to the wooden bar before him, he must have fallen to the ground. The sensation throughout the court was great; it was very evident that now the truth was coming to light. The dagger, on being examined, was proved, by Sabina and the abbot, to belong to the late baron. The monk's garb had now to be explained.

" Whoever is the murderer," the legate observed, " he is a monk? If the gown cannot be identified, let the person who has the care of the simple dress of the monks, attend."

The monk was in court; he had spoken in favour of seeing Albert on the day of the murder. On stepping forward, the legate desired him to look at the gown, and state if he knew anything of it. Again the court was all anxiety, and Albert gave up all for lost. The monk declared that he could come to no conclusion, further than he conceived it to be a dress belonging to the convent; but, among so many, in was impossible to say to whom it might have belonged. Their garments were not marked. Each monk had a cell to himself, so that their clothes could never be mixed. The opinion of the court and legate was now not in favour of Albert. He saw it, and his firmness and presence of mind were put to the test. Addressing the legate, he delivered himself thus :—" Your grace, and you my lords spiritual and temporal, must, I am convinced, see the severity of my fate, that thus places me in a situation I do not merit. I am exposed to the hatred of mankind, and labouring under the weight of an imputed crime. Because I had the unhappiness to offend the baron, I am accused of his murder. A person who has been injured by the baron seeks revenge; a body of soldiers are in the neighbourhood. He assumes the habit of one of these men, commits the murder, and buries the dress. A man in the company, or legion, has been punished by the baron; and, while smarting under his hurts, vows revenge. The man is now taken up; would it be right that man should be killed ?"

" No, no," exclaimed a hundred voices.

" The case is similar here," continued Albert; " the dress of the monk is easier to be procured than that of the soldier. Then it is proved that every monk has his dress. I have my own, yet I am singled out. I must have committed the murder, because the baron and I quarrelled. Is this just? Is it not more likely that one who had expectations would destroy him, to render the road to fortune more easy to attain. Yet I am the murderer! Did two men never quarrel yet? Did a man never say that in the heat of passion, which he never did perform or ever mean? If this be so, then am I guilty; but if you allow not such things, then am I the murderer."

As he sat down, a tumultuous shout proclaimed him innocent, and the legate confirmed it; but that day did a deadly injury to Cyril, by pointing the suspicion of the court to him. Albert saved himself, but so deeply was it impressed on the minds of all, that Cyril was guilty, that he directly received notice to quit the castle. Not a soul would take him in. Even Jocelyn the abbot, refused to aid him, and but for the little tailor, Pierce Gherkin who swore that the lad had nothing to do with it, he must have perished. He took the hapless youth in, saying,—

" They may talk as they like, but for all I'm such a fool, I know there was more than one monk, or two monks. The legate's too fond of his own sort—I'd have tried every one of them, as well as Master Albert. Holy poker, I beg his pardon, Father Ernest. I know he was innocent, but I'll be d—d if you are guilty."

The good little tailor was never known to have swore an oath before, so that the accusing spirit would not believe the sound, and passed the sinner by. Albert had not positively refused to assist Cyril, but he had avoided him since the trial. Albert had made it his business to attain a high character for charity, and virtue, and holiness; his piety was the theme of every tongue. It would not then have done for him to be seen relieving one who was despised, and suspected,—his piety would suffer by it.

Sabina had fixed to go into a convent. But what is not love? Albert had been proved innocent to her whose heart was predisposed to believe him innocent; but Jocelyn, the best of the cloistered school, whose home was heaven, and whose children were mankind, felt a weight at his heart—a mistrust, as the French say—a presentiment that all was not right with Albert. The change that had taken place was unnatural; the abbot doubted, feared, and suspected; Sabina gave herself up to grief, and kept her suite of rooms, leaving the care of the castle to the warder, the new castellan being also castellan of Walmer Castle, and not inhabiting Richborough, courteously offered Sabina to remain till her grief should be abated, when she would repair to St. Genevieve, the manorial mansion—Richborough, like Walmer and Dover, being a military station and government possession ; so that an officer took command of the military there stationed.

Lord de Broan, the commandant of Walmer and Richborough, passed much of his time at the latter place, striving to rouse Sabina from her melancholy. He was a merry old knight, and a relative, by marriage, to the Fitzormond family. His son, Hildebrand, whom he left in command of the military at Richborough, was a fine young man, and was a source of perpetual misery to Albert. The world, which loves to make matches, had united him and Sabina already by hearsay ; and that they doted upon each other, and were inseparable, was in the mouth of every one. Still, Albert disguised his sentiments, pretending to rejoice that Sabina had found a good protector, and also launched forth in praises of the young man ; often lamenting that he was not able to see Sabina, that he might urge her to value his merits as they ought to be estimated, and in Hildebrand de Broan, restore the hopes of those who wished to see the daughter of the Fitzormond continue the race.

Time passed on, and in Stonar and Richborough, with their vicinity, the name of Father Ernest was sounded with praises far and near—so good, so pious ! Was there a person ill, snow, hail, or rain detained not Father Earnest. To the poor he was indeed a good Samaritan. The rest of the monks were thought of but little, in comparison to Father Ernest ; and even the holy abbot himself, though certainly one of the best and noblest-hearted of mankind, was little thought of by the admirers of Father Ernest.

People knelt and blessed him as he passed ; their sons and daughters invited him to their tables, while their children strewed rushes and flowrets before the monk of St. Mark, as he was called, giving him the individuality, as having, in their opinion, merited it by his more than mortal piety. So was it with him, when one night he was summoned to attend the bedside of a dying brother. When he reached the cell, he found it was Father John, the same who, at the trial, had come forward as the keeper of the stores, wardrobe, &c. He found him in a very bad state. The leech had given him up, and the aged monk was preparing for his transit from this world of woe. He had for a length of time—indeed, ever since the trial—taken a great liking to Albert, and was one of the many that looked upon him as the essence of sanctity. Alas ! they who believed thus, saw not the midnight orgies of Albert and his bacchanalian brethren.

The good Jocelyn was laid up by gout, and the infirmities attendant on a wealthy old age, where the subject has ever lived in luxury and comfort.

The convent was very richly endowed—so much so, that the Abbot of St. Mark would have despised the paltry benefice of the bishoprick of Rochester, which, to the present day, is one of the poorest of that class. The worthy abbot would, therefore, live well ; he enjoyed the pleasures of the table with the elder and principal monks, while the others were invited to dine with the superior in turn, like the middies of a man-of-war ; but the regular dinner was held in the refectory, where the meal was in the style of monkish abstinence, which they amply made up for by their soirees at each other's cells. Jocelyn was confined to his room, and under the direction of the monk Antoine, or Antonio, or, as he was more familiarly called by the lower classes, Father Antony, the fraternity were suffered to indulge in all sorts of debauchery, when, with closed doors, they were hid from worldly ken.

Albert was the prime mover and chief of all these midnight orgies ; yet, when called to attend to his saintly duties, no one so ready to attend. Therefore, though called from his midnight revels, he promptly attended the dying man, who desired that all should quit the cell but Father Ernest, to whose ear he wished to breathe his last confession.

When all were retired, he took the hand of Albert, and said,—

" I have been a wretch all my lifetime, scraping up gold which I cannot now take with me. Listen, holy father—listen to—

The Confession of Father John.

My father was a fisherman, and at an early age I was made the companion of his dangerous occupation. We lived in a poor cottage on the beach, directly under a huge cliff, and yet ourselves a good distance from the sands below. The domicile would have been despised by the traveller and the citizen, but I thought it a paradise. I have looked at it as we returned of an afternoon, or at evening sunset, and thought, as the sun shone on the whitewashed walls, that the castles and mansions of the rich that I had seen never looked half so pleasant. I was an only child, and was loved by my mother as dearly as I loved her. My father was of a surly, taciturn humour; would often be out with me for a whole day and never speak a single word to me, a child of ten years of age; but if I committed any error, would give me a violent blow with a rope's end. If I cried I got it double, and if I did not cry he beat me for being a hardened young dog, that would be sure to come to the gallows. When drunk, he was brutality personified. Going out one morning, to take up some lobster pots that lay at the mouth of the river, I was asked by a gentleman to put him on board of a xebec that lay off the headland, for which, after I had done, he gave me a groat, the first piece of money I ever had of my own. All day I kept taking it out to admire, and in the evening I buried it, getting up by daylight the next morning to see if my treasure was safe. My whole and sole thought was now given to the accumulation of money, and when I was fifteen I had accumulated above forty shillings of sterling money. My father found out that I possessed this sum, and having occasion for it—for we were wretchedly poor,—insisted on my giving it to him, which I promised to do the next morning. In the night I went to all the places where I had buried it, for I placed it in several spots, lest, being found out, I should lose the whole of my immense treasure at once. Having collected it, and put on the best of my clothes, I set off to seek my fortune in a strange wide world, sooner than give up the idol of my soul. I walked all night as quickly as my feet would carry me, turning in as many directions as I could, that my father might not overtake me; and, as to the way I went, all places were alike to me, who had never been five miles from the place I was born in (at least, on land) in my life. About five o'clock, being tired at the rate I had travelled, I sat down on a bank by the roadside, and began to think what was to be done. Never was so unlicked a cub as I was; I knew no more of the world than a tom-cat. 'Tis true, I had a fortune in my pocket, but how long would that last? I knew not how to work, except in pulling an oar or drawing a net; but I thought I could soon learn. While I was sitting thus, an old man, with very white hair, came and sat by me. He said he had come many miles, and was going to find a daughter that lived at Coventry, but that he feared he should never reach it. Questioning me about where I was going, I told him my parents were dead, and that I was going to look for work somewhere, and I asked him if Coventry was a good place to get work in. He told me he was a Coventry man, and made no doubt, if we were there, he could get me something to do among the farmers; but that it was a long way, and asked me if I had got any money. I told him that I hadn't a doit, for I was cunning enough for that, and had even the precaution, before I set off, to sew my money in the lining of my doublet. He said he had a charge of money about him, that if I had a mind to help him along, he would pay for my food on the road; and if anything happened to him, and I would take the money to his daughter, I might keep half for my trouble and honesty; that the sale of his clothes and little valuables he had about him would pay for his funeral; that I seemed a nice honest lad, and he was glad he had met with me for both our sakes. He then showed me a bag of money, among which were several gold coins—things I had never seen before; they were French or Norman pieces of money, such being most common in circulation, for we had no gold coinage of our own. I thought that he must be some prince or king in disguise, to have so much money, and my respect increased accordingly, such veneration did I hold money or the possessor of it in.

Wherever we stopped, he told the people that I was his son, and I got much praise and a good deal of drink, which I got very fond of, for being so good to my old father. It would take us three weeks to get to Coventry, I found. At night, when I lay down again, I thought of getting the old man's money from him again, and even dreamed of it, and talked so much in my sleep that I let it out, and it alarmed the old man so much that he gave me no beer or spirits the next day, and told me so many stories of thieves and murderers being hung and broke on the wheel, that it quite frightened me from my intention.

See p. 93.

We passed the gibbet of a murderer, with part o. the body hanging in irons, which had nearly frightened me to death—indeed, I swooned away, which made the old man very frightened, and induced him to give me more beer than ever; but the weight of him, through two days, had so tired me, that the next morning he was forced to walk as before, and at evening we were so far from any village or house that he said we should be obliged to lay under a tree all night. Now, thought I, is the time to rob the old man ; and it so laid hold of me, that when he fell asleep, which he soon did through sheer fatigue, I put my hand in his bosom, and drew forth the bag of gold I so much coveted. In exultation at my fancied success, I could not refrain, notwithstanding the danger there was of the old man awaking, from pouring the glittering contents upon the ground, and feasting my eyes upon the treasure.

The jingling of the money aroused the old man, and with a cry of alarm he rushed upon me. In the struggle that ensued, he was thrown to the ground, and then, in my anxiety to secure the prize which was now within my grasp, I caught up a large stone which was lying close at hand, and dashed out his brains.

At that time I had no remorse for the dreadful deed I had committed—the rapture I experienced at being the possessor of so much gold, was so great that I was blind as to the guilt which I had incurred. I begged my way to London, for I would not venture to break in upon my treasure ; and, when I arrived there, I sought about for some means whereby I might invest my ill-gotten gains to advantage. I was successful, and I went on from year to year, adding daily to my store. But retribution came at last, and I was dishonoured in the person of my wife by a favoured guest. By accident I discovered their perfidy, and I slew them both—my wife and her paramour. Then, in my lonely chamber, the recollections of the terrible past would come upon me—the form of that helpless old man whose life I had taken, night after night, hovered round my couch, with his silver hair floating over his pale face, all dabbled with blood, and his shrieks of agony would be echoed by a thousand voices, that filled my chamber with most soul-thrilling sounds.

At length, driven by remorse and despair, I bestowed my wealth upon the Abbey of St. Mark, resolved, by a life of penance and prayer to atone for the past.

The strength of the monk, as he uttered these words, appeared to be exhausted, and he sank back upon his pallet. Father Ernest hastily pronounced his absolution, and after administering the rites required by the church, he quitted the cell, meditating upon the strange chances which had thrown together such a number of men in holy brotherhood, scarce one of whom was clear from the guilt of shedding blood. In less than an hour afterwards, one of the lay brothers, who had been in attendance upon Father John, came to say that he was dead.

As was usual when one of the fraternity died, the whole of the monks remained in their cells to pray, during the whole of the night, for the repose of the soul of the departed. Father Ernest certainly confined himself to his cell, but no holy aspiration passed his lips, no fervent invocation to the Great One on high for mercy for the deceased, came from the heart of the father. He sat immersed in thought—and that, too, of the most criminal nature. His soul sickened at the restraint imposed upon him by the monastic dress, and he longed to throw it off, and again to mingle with the world and its pleasures. Sabina, too, more lovely than ever, floated before his excited imagination, and as the thought that she was lost to him for ever crossed his mind, he started from his seat and paced the floor with disordered steps, while expressions of the most feverish impatience burst from him.

"Fool, fool! that I was!" he exclaimed, in a paroxysm of despair; "why did I ever pronounce those vows which have cut me off from the world for ever, without deadening those passions of my soul which burn so fiercely within me? Wealth, power, love, all are as naught to me while I wear these accursed garments. And Sabina, too! I am lost to her for ever—for ever!"

The last words seemed to echo through the apartment as if taken up by numberless invisible speakers.

"For ever—for ever!"

Father Ernest started, and glanced in terror around him. There was a dark shadow upon the wall at the further end of the cell, although the moon was shining full upon it. It had no substance, and its indistinctness prevented the monk distinguishing what it was. For a few moments he remained gazing at it in terror, and each moment it seemed to increase in distinctness and density, and then the form of the Ocean Fiend, in all his terrible native grandeurs, stood before him. The pale moonbeams, which had hitherto shone with a strong yet subdued light, changed to a blood red, and fell in a full flood upon the ghastly features of the fiend, while the scales on his body glittered in that fearful light like molten gold.

Father Ernest sank upon his knees before that dread being, and would have hid his face in his hands, but a spell seemed to be upon him, and he felt it impossible to remove his eyes from the fixed and stone-like gaze of the Sea-fiend.

"Man of blood," at length spoke the fiend, "I know thy thoughts. *I* can free thee from the thraldom which now enslaves thee—I alone can help thee. Speak; wilt thou accept my aid?"

The monk trembled at the sound of the voice of the fiend, but the words he uttered seemed to print themselves in living, burning fire upon his brain.

"I can free thee—I can free thee!" came to his heart in such wondrous power, that he almost felt tempted to accept the proffered aid, even at the risk of the terrible forfeit which he knew was the condition of that aid. Then came the thought that it might be a dream, similar to those he had had before; but there stood the Sea-fiend, in all his fearful majesty, and he could doubt no longer.

"Wealth, power, love!" murmured the fiend, in a low, thrilling tone, that seemed like some distant echo. "Mortal, is he who reigns in the depths of the ocean to aid thee? Speak thy wishes."

The monk seemed to be suddenly endowed with a supernatural energy, and throwing himself at the feet of the spirit, he exclaimed,—

"Give me but wealth, power, and Sabina, and I am thine, only thine, for ever."

"Thou must earn these for thyself," was the reply. "Be mine the task to provide the opportunity for their attainment. Stretch forth thy hand."

With a shudder the monk obeyed, and he felt his wrist grasped by a hand cold as ice, yet when it was released there were marks upon it as though it had been seared by a red-hot iron. The most fearful agony ran through his whole frame, and he drew himself up, as if every limb were convulsed with pain. When he again looked up, his cell was deserted, save by himself, and the moonbeams were shining calm and silvery as before the dread visitation. Ernest drew his hand across his eyes, as if to convince himself that he was not labouring under a delusion, but then his gaze fell upon the marks on his wrist, and he felt persuaded that he had indeed made a compact with one who had both the power and the will to enforce its fulfilment.

The rest of the night was passed by the monk in triumphant reflections upon the glorious future that lay before him, and daybreak still found him seated at his casement, lost in thought. This was suddenly interrupted by the loud tolling of the alarm-bell of the abbey, and on hastening, filled with wonder, to the refectory, whither all the monks appeared to be hurrying, Father Ernest found that the abbot Jocelyn had just been found dead in his bed, without any marks of violence on his person. Ernest started when he received this information, for he could not help coupling this sudden occurrence with the promise of opportunity given him by the fiend; and, when the excitement had somewhat died away, he was still more agreeably surprised by receiving an intimation from the brotherhood that their choice had unanimously fallen upon him as successor to the deceased abbot, provided it received the confirmation of the higher authorities. This confirmation, after the lapse of a few weeks, arrived, and then, amidst the most imposing ceremonies, Albert Durand, or rather Father Ernest, was installed Abbot of St. Mark's.

Here, then, were both power and wealth placed in his hands, and Ernest at once proceeded to make that use of both which did not tend to sustain the character for supposed sanctity, which had hitherto been attributed to him. As he gave the most unrestrained licence to his own passions, so did he permit those under his control to follow his example; and, from the quiet abode of peace that it was, under the pious rule of the late abbot, Jocelyn, it became the scene of the most riotous orgies; the vaulted passages of the abbey rang with shouts and laughter instead of the solemn chant of praises; and more like a haunt of banditti did that holy place become.

The abbot's love of Sabina had increased since his elevation to his new dignity, but what it gained in intensity, it had lost in purity, and he had made a resolution to attempt to obtain possession of her person by force or stratagem, for he felt convinced that she would shrink from him with horror were he to press his suit in his supposed holy character.

The immense wealth of the convent placed at his disposal the services of many who were ever willing to give them for hire, and assembling a goodly number of these hired desperadoes, he, in disguise, headed them himself, and once more grasping a sword, he led them forth under the cover of darkness. The purpose he had in view was an unexpected attack upon Richborough Castle, for the purpose of securing Sabina. The scheme was a suggestion of the fiend—the opportunity was offered—he felt—he knew that he must succeed.

The band were soon under the deep shadow of the walls of Richborough, and with cautious footsteps Ernest stole forward, to discover a mode of effecting an entrance. High up on the wall, at a spot where it was deemed inaccessible from the precipitous nature of the rock on which the stronghold was built, was posted a solitary man-at-arms. His figure was clearly distinguishable, as the moon threw a strong light upon his brightly polished morion, and glanced fitfully on the shining cross-bow which he carried.

Ernest knew that the walls were to be gained from where he stood, as, many a time, when a boy, he had climbed them by a path known only to himself; but this sentinel was an obstacle which he knew not how to overcome, and in a voice of passion he called upon the fiend to aid him.

The abbot fancied he heard a rustling of pinions in the air, and thought that the melancholy dash of the waves on the strand below sounded louder than before. He felt that he was not mistaken—he had not called for aid in vain. In a few moments the sentinel, who had been leaning on the edge of the ramparts, gazing upon the broad expanse of ocean spread before him, gradually bent his head upon his breast, and then, from his immoveable attitude, it became apparent that he slept.

Ernest returned to his men, and cautioning them to remain where they were until they were joined by him again, he commenced the ascent of the rock, on reaching the summit of which it was comparatively easy to climb the low wall which there guarded the castle. The sentinel slept soundly, and Ernest at once determined, if it were at all possible, to reach the great gates, and to admit his band through a small postern which opened in one of them.

The way was well known to the abbot, and he proceeded hastily through the long passages which led to the gates. A dreary silence reigned throughout the vast building, and it seemed as though the whole of the inhabitants of the castle, at other times so vigilant and watchful, were now wrapped in a supernatural slumber. The usually noisy guard-room was now silent as a chamber of death, and the men lay grouped about the room in sleep.

To join his friends without, and to order them to follow him, was but the work of a moment, and then the whole party entered the court. First placing a few sentinels, and enjoining the strictest silence, Ernest then, accompanied by three followers, sought the chamber in which Sabina slept. He knew the way too well of old to have forgotten it now, and the corridor on to which it opened was soon gained. The door of a chamber, at some small distance from that of Sabina, stood slightly open, and he could see that a taper was burning in a sconce near the hearth. Motioning to his men to remain where they were, the abbot seemed drawn by an irresistible power into that apartment.

On a low couch, at the further end of the room, reclined the form of a young and handsome man. Ernest recognised it at once—it was that of Hildebrand de Broan, the son of the commandant of Walmer, to whom rumour had given the heart of Sabina.

The monk paused, with a gloomy look, before the sleeping man, and his hand unconsciously wandered to his bosom, and grasped the hilt of his glass dagger.

"Strike—strike deep!" murmured a well known voice close to his ear, "and rid thyself of a dangerous rival."

The abbot turned suddenly, but a fleeting shadow on the wall was the only thing that caught his eye; nor was the least sound to be heard, save the heavy, deep-breathing of the sleeper before him. He gazed upon the handsome features of the young man; and as he did so, a world of hate seemed to grow within his breast. A sudden passion seized him, and drawing the blade from its place of concealment, it flashed for a moment in the light of the taper, and then was buried in the heart of De Broan. The blow was sure, and, with scarce a sound on his lips, the soul of the young knight had fled. A slight, hissing laugh stole through that silent chamber, and, with a heart chilled with horror at the deed, Ernest rushed from the room.

In the dim light given by a lamp carried by one of the men, his agitation was unremarked, and he hastily hurried to the chamber of Sabina. To the great surprise of the party, voices were heard within, and they halted for a moment to listen. The abbot at once recognized one of them to be Sabina, and as the person she was addressing, from the voice, appeared to be a female, he felt but little doubt that it was one of her maidens. With a hasty movement, Ernest threw open the door of the room, and stood, like a spirit of evil, before her whom he professed to love."

Sabina was kneeling before a crucifix, and, as she raised her face towards heaven, with her masses of dark hair falling over her shoulders, and her small hands clasped as in prayer, Ernest thought he had never seen her look so beautiful; and if he had ever entertained a thought of remorse, it was at once driven from his mind, and his determination to possess her became stronger than ever.

"Sabina," he exclaimed, in as gentle a tone as he could assume.

The maiden started to her feet, and gazed at the intruder in mingled astonishment and alarm. Then the pride of her sex came to her aid, and she asked, in an indignant tone, as she recognized the person who addressed her, —

"Father Ernest, why are you here, and at this hour?"

Ernest turned to the men who had followed him into the room, and beckoned them to await without. They obeyed, and then he advanced towards Sabina.

"Sabina," he again said, "have the feelings with which you once regarded the youthful Albert Durand no place now within your breast? He loved you when, in years gone by, he wore the plumed cap, and carried the glittering sword. He loves you now, even though he wears the garments of a monk, and carries no weapon save the breviary. You can—you must relieve that love; for think not, fair maiden, that the cold walls of a monastery have deadened the passions that have found a home within my breast. Meditation on your beauties have but inflamed them, and my love for you, sweet Sabina, has increased a thousand fold."

"Oh! monstrous blasphemy!" she exclaimed; "is it thus one of God's servants should speak? Leave me, if you would not have me curse your memory. Another moment, and I will rouse the garrison."

"Spare your efforts, fair Sabina. The whole of the garrison lie in a state of supernatural slumber, from which no efforts of yours can arouse them."

The unfortunate lady sank on to a seat, and wept bitterly, while he continued,—

"I have the means of procuring both wealth and power, Sabina; indeed, I have them both. Fly with me, and we will live only for love. Refuse to comply with my request, and, by the powers of darkness, to whom I am bound, I swear you shall be mine by force; nor shall you ever again pass the walls of St. Mark. Say, Sabina, will you leave this place with me?"

"Rather welcome death itself," almost shrieked the maiden, "than thy now loathsome embraces. Oh, Albert!" she added, wringing her hands imploringly, "for that name is still dear to me, how fearfully changed art thou! For the sake of what you once were, I will save you the guilt of the crime you have contemplated."

With these words, Sabina rose hastily, and before Ernest could prevent her, she passed through a small door which led by a narrow staircase to the summit of one of the towers.

The abbot darted after her in alarm, and he heard her hurried footsteps echoing above him as she rapidly ascended. "What could be her object?" he asked himself; and he feared to answer that question. He increased his speed, and as he gained the opening that led on to the summit, he saw the light form of Sabina in strong relief against the moonlit sky, as she stood on one of the battlements.

"Hold, for mercy's sake, hold, Sabina," he cried, in a tone of agony, as he beheld the marble countenance of the fair girl turned in terror upon him.

"Forego your purpose, then, monster," was the reply, in a tone of voice so different from what it had been, that the abbot scarce recognised it. "Forego your purpose, if you would save me."

"I cannot—you must—you shall be mine," returned the monk, with an intensity of passion that overcame all prudence.

Throwing her arms aloft, the wretched girl hesitated but for a moment, and then she precipitated herself from that fearful height. Ernest saw the flutter of her white garments as she disappeared, and, with a cry of horror, he fell senseless on the stones.

When the abbot recovered from his insensibility, sounds the most discordant were ringing in his ears. The shouts of men were heard in every direction below; and what appeared to be the rushing of flames, and the crackling of burning timber, came distinctly to his astonished ears. He advanced to the edge of the battlement, and looked beneath him. The whole of that part of·the castle from which rose the turret on which he stood, was one mass of flames, and the clouds of whirling smoke that rose upwards, nearly blinded him. Then he suddenly recollected that as he rushed from the room in which the murdered De Broan lay, he had overturned the taper on to the rush strewn floor, and thus had he built a snare for his own destruction.

The abbot rushed down the staircase, but when he entered the room where he had had the interview with Sabina, the smoke and flame were so great, that he was forced to retreat, and with a mind bordering on distraction, he again mounted the turret. In his compact with the fiend, he had received no assurance of personal safety, and he saw that the moment had now arrived when he was to pay the fearful penalty for his alliance with the agents of the lower world.

The atmosphere now breathed by the abbot was suffocating, blinding—the very stones beneath his feet seemed red-hot—his head reeled—his eyes grew dizzy, and, as he sank to the ground, he became conscious of a burning grasp upon his throat. Then the fearful sound of pinions, which he had so often heard and trembled at before, came upon his bewildered senses—he felt himself carried up—up to an inconceivable height, and consciousness deserted him.

*   *   *   *   *

At the first signs of the fire, the men who were waiting in the corridor the appearance of the abbot, quitted their post, and joined their comrades in the outer court, and the whole body made an instant retreat from the castle, leaving the inmates to their fate. Several of the guards, however, broke through their lethargy, the alarm was given, and every effort was made to stop the progress of the fire, but in vain. The burning castle became the funeral pyre of the body of De Broan; and when the mangled body of Sabina was found at the foot of the cliffs, it was supposed that she had perished in attempting to escape.

In the height of the conflagration, the attention of the garrison was attracted by fearful sounds that came from the summit of one of the turrets, and when all eyes were turned in the direction, two dark forms were seen to rise from the roof—the one in the grasp of the other—and soar through the air in the direction of the ocean.

On they went with the swiftness of the meteor; then suddenly a dark cloud enveloped them both, and when it cleared away, no traces were to be seen of either the Sea-fiend, or the guilty, blood-stained Abbot of St. Mark's.

THE END,

www.ingramcontent.com/pod-product-compliance
Lightning Source LLC
Chambersburg PA
CBHW081212170626
46811CB00010B/3254